TOGA'S DEMONS

SATAN'S LEGACY MC

ANDI RHODES

BLUE JOURNEY PUBLISHING

Also by Andi Rhodes

Broken Rebel Brotherhood

Broken Souls

Broken Innocence

Broken Boundaries

Broken Rebel Brotherhood: Complete Series Box set

Broken Rebel Brotherhood: Next Generation

Broken Hearts

Broken Wings

Broken Mind

Bastards and Badges

Stark Revenge

Slade's Fall

Jett's Guard

Soulless Kings MC

Fender

Joker

Piston

Greaser

Riker

Trainwreck

Squirrel

Gibson

Satan's Legacy MC

Snow's Angel

Toga's Demons

Magic's Torment

SATAN'S LEGACY MC

DENVER, CO CHAPTER

**What the patch binds together,
let no force tear apart.
Satan's Legacy now and forever.**

PROLOGUE
TOGA

Eight years ago...

"You're seriously leaving?"

I shift my gaze from the duffel bag on my bed to Fallon, my step sister. She's fidgeting with her hands, picking at her hot pink nail polish and letting the scraps fall into her lap. After three years of living in the same house, I recognize it as her way of ignoring her fear.

"I told you I was getting the fuck outta here as soon as possible," I remind her.

"Right." She leans back against the headboard and huffs out a breath. "But I thought..."

I push my duffel aside and sit down next to her. The words that fly out of my mouth have the potential to kill me because they're designed to hurt her. That's the only way I can leave... my hometown, my mom, *her*.

"You thought what? That I'd change my mind just because we kissed a few weeks ago?"

If I'm being honest, that kiss is the one and only thing

1

that could get me to stay. I like Fallon, more than I should. But she's my step sister and too young.

Fallon's eyes widen, and it isn't more than a few seconds before her bottom lip quivers and a tear spills down her cheek. My instinct is to reach out to her and offer comfort. That's always my instinct where she's concerned. Ever since my mom married her dad, ever since I walked into this house of horrors, I've wanted to shield Fallon from the abuse, the hatred, the wrath of Ben.

Ben.

Dear old stepdad.

Piece of shit who preys on those weaker than him.

"I always knew you were an ass, but cruel? That, I didn't see coming."

"Remember that the next time you think you know someone."

I rise from the bed and move to the dresser to start sorting through its content. I'm limited on space because my only mode of transportation is the used Harley I bought after saving for almost three years. The hunk of metal is all I could afford.

Raised voices are muffled by the door, but I don't have to make out the words to know what they're saying: 'You're a whore', 'I shouldn't have married you', 'Please stop', 'I'll do whatever you want'. It's been the same loop, screamed over and over again, for the last three and a half years.

That's when Mom and Ben got married. He's her fourth husband, and she traded modesty for money, but the money also came with violence and terror. I'd take modesty over that any day.

All it took was one date with a man she met online, a man who saw her desperation to feel anything good, and the rest, as they say, is history. My mom came home from their fourth date only to announce she was getting married. I wish I could say I was surprised, but ever since my father died, she's been impulsive when it comes to men. It's like she's chasing the connection she had with my dad. Unfortunately, no one can give her what she wants. No one will ever compare.

Somewhere in the house, glass shatters. I glance at Fallon out of the corner of my eye, and she's now poised on the edge of the bed, like she's debating whether or not she should try and break up the fight.

"Don't."

Fallon lifts her eyes to mine. "We can't just sit here and do nothing," she insists.

I absently reach up and touch the bruising around my eye. "Yeah, we can."

She shoots to her feet and stomps to the door. I rush to block her and wrap my hands around her biceps. She struggles against me, but she's a tiny little thing, and it gets her nowhere.

"Let me go!"

"No." I push her back toward the mattress and force her to sit down. "Fallon, you know what will happen if you go out there. You'll be his next target."

She waves dismissively. "I'm used to it."

I drop my hands and heave a sigh. "Yeah, well, you shouldn't be." I rub the side of my nose and spit out the words I told myself I wouldn't, under any circumstances, utter. "Do you wanna go with me?"

As soon as the words are out, my brain scrambles with ways to call them back. Fortunately for me, Fallon is either too scared to go or stupid enough to stay.

"You know I can't do that," she argues. "I've got two years of school left and, as bad as Dad is, it's his money that pays for private school. How the hell am I even going to graduate, let alone from a good school, if I'm on the road with you?"

"I don't know," I admit. "But isn't—"

"See." Fallon rises to her feet and begins to pace. "That's just it... you never think about anything. You just get a whim and act on it."

Little does she know, I think about things a lot. And me leaving isn't a whim. I've been thinking about it every day for the last three years, ever since the first time I tried to step in and protect my mom from Ben. All I got for my trouble was a broken arm and a juvenile record.

The thing about Ben is, he has connections. Combine those connections with his money and he'll keep getting away with whatever the hell he wants. People will keep getting hurt, and some day, he'll take it too far and hurt will turn into death.

Fallon stomps to the door and, out of habit, I strain to listen for the sound of fighting. When I hear none, I don't bother stopping her from leaving. Besides, she's safe... for now. After one of Ben's rants is the safest time to be in this house because he's calm, like he got the rage out of his system and can now breathe.

Fallon opens the door but pauses before stepping into the hallway and turns to me. "You've obviously made up your mind." She lowers her eyes a moment and tears spill down her cheek. I force my internal shields in place and try to ignore them. "Just remember, while you're out running like a coward, your mom and I will still be here, on the receiving end of whatever my dad dishes out. And regardless of how much he beats us down or tries to eviscerate our

4

memories of you, we won't stop loving you. We may hate you, but we'll still love you."

She turns back toward the door and steps through, holding onto the frame with loose fingers. "Have a good life David," she says over her shoulder and then walks down the hall.

That's where you're wrong, kid.

There is no love in this house. Hell, my mom stopped loving me years ago, after my father died. She said that I reminded her of him. Don't get me wrong, she's not a bad mother, but after marrying Ben, she's not anything anymore. An empty shell of the woman who gave birth to me, loved me through the first nine years of my life.

And Fallon? She doesn't love me. Not even like a brother. She's enamored with me, with the idea of me. But there's no love there. Maybe, in another life, another time, but not in this one. We're both too defined by our parents, by the craziness we've been thrust into.

Shoving those thoughts into a box deep inside my mind, I finish going through my room, grabbing anything I can, anything that means something to me. I force it all into the duffel bag and struggle to get the zipper closed. The thing is bursting at the seams.

I give the room one last look before exiting and making my way downstairs to the front door. Just as I start to twist the knob and escape, my mom's voice stops me.

"You can't leave me."

I can hear the pain in her words, the devastation. The problem is, I can't be sure it's because I'm leaving and not from the knock-down, drag-out between her and Ben. Either way, I can't stay.

"I can't stay," I say without turning to face her.

"What am I supposed to do without you? You're my baby."

I spin to face her, anger flowing through my veins and burning like acid.

"I'm not your baby," I counter. "In case you haven't noticed, I grew up. And I can't stay here, Mom. Not with him."

Her face contorts. "Oh, but I can?"

I thrust my hand through my hair. "I'm not going to argue with you. I've tried to convince you to leave him hundreds of times, and each time, you choose him over yourself, over me. I'm done."

"That's not fair."

I lock eyes with her. "You're right, Mom. It isn't fair."

I ignore her pleas with me to stay, her hands clawing at me to stop, and leave the house. I rush down the steps, toward the circular driveway where I parked the Harley. Before I even get to it, I push my arms through the straps of the duffel and sling it onto my back.

When I straddle the bike, I glance back, half expecting to see my mom standing there, but the porch is empty. I let my gaze travel to each window and stop when I come to Fallon's.

There, peeking from behind the curtains, is my step sister. I watch as she swipes her cheeks, and a piece of my heart shatters. Leaving my mom is difficult, but she made her choice. Leaving Fallon is unbearable, because she didn't choose the life she was born into.

She's choosing it now... and all because of education.

I lift my hand in a half-hearted wave, but she doesn't wave back. Fine, no sweat off my back. Shifting my gaze away from her, I face forward and look down the lane that extends from the driveway, the road that will provide the initial path to my freedom.

I have no idea what the future holds for me. But I *do* know, it can't be any worse than the past I'm leaving behind.

CHAPTER 1

FALLON

PRESENT DAY...

I flip through the mail I picked up off my floor when I stepped inside my apartment.

Bill.

Bill.

Credit card offer.

Junk.

Bill.

Not in the mood to deal with the bills, I toss them on the side table and carry the rest to the trash. Then I move to the fridge and grab the bottle of wine I opened last night.

I fill my wine glass and set the bottle on the counter before walking to my bedroom and kicking out of my heels. Flexing my feet, I dig my toes into the plush rug and savor the luxuriousness of it. Knowing that I could get lost in the way it feels, I cross the room and set my glass on the dresser.

My dress falls to the floor after I peel it from my body. Next, I take off my bra and panties, leaving them in a heap with the dress. I make my way to the attached bathroom, grabbing my wine glass as I do. I turn on the water to start filling the tub and then add a bath bomb before deciding I'm going to need more wine.

I run out to the kitchen naked, snatch the bottle off the counter, and race back to the bathroom. I set the bottle on the floor next to the tub and pick up my glass, holding the stem between my fingers as I dip one foot in the water to check the temperature. As I step into the tub, I adjust the water to make it a little warmer and then submerge myself in vanilla scented bubbles until only my head and the hand holding the wine glass poke out.

Ah, just what I needed after a long day.

It started out as any normal day. I woke up, drank coffee, got ready, and then left for work. I was supposed to interview several individuals for positions in the non-profit I'm starting, Source of Love, but two out of the six didn't show up, one sucked, one was iffy, and the last two were great. We're officially set to open in two months, and I'm afraid things won't be ready in time. All I want is to offer a safe haven and support to kids who've suffered from abuse at the hands of their parents and there's a very real concern that staffing issues will prevent me from doing that.

Add that to my ever-growing list of fears.

Lifting my glass to my lips, I realize it's empty and reach out to grab the bottle and fill it. Just as I swallow the first sip, my cell phone rings from the other room. My muscles tense when the sound of *All Nightmare Long* by Metallica fills the air. That's the song I gave *him* as a ringtone. It serves as a reminder that I can never let my guard down where he's concerned.

Any feelings of calm the bubble bath and wine provided disappear as quickly as the song ends. Not that I won't hear it again. Dear old Dad has a habit of calling until I pick up.

I've had as many as forty-seven missed calls in an hour and that was only two days ago. He's on a rampage for some reason, and when that happens, I'm always his last stop on that particular crazy train.

After the fifth call, I resign myself to no longer being able to relax. I climb out of the tub and set my glass on the counter so I can grab a towel and wrap it around my body. Surprisingly, after three more calls, they stop completely. I can't help but wonder why, but I push the question out of my mind, telling myself it doesn't matter. He stopped, and that's all I care about.

I grab my phone out of the pocket of my dress and, without bothering to throw clothes on, crawl under the sheets and snuggle in for the night. I'm exhausted and don't have the slightest motivation to do anything but sleep.

How much time passes, I have no idea. I managed to drift off, but the pounding on my door pulls me from my dreams. I kick off the covers and grab my cell from the nightstand to glance at the time. Four in the morning. Crossing the room, I snag the robe hanging next to the closet and put it on. No doubt whoever is at the door doesn't need to see me in my birthday suit.

The pounding continues... incessantly.

"I'm coming, I'm coming," I mumble as I pad to the door.

Why on earth would the doorman let someone up at this time of night? I pay good money for the security this building provides, and right now, I don't feel like I'm getting my money's worth.

Unlocking the door, I yank it open. My cell slips through my fingers and thuds against the floor.

"It's about time you opened the fucking door," my dad

slurs. He stumbles past me, and I can smell the booze wafting off of him.

Great. He's on a rampage and a bender.

As he makes his way to the kitchen, no doubt looking for booze, I press the red button on the panel next to the door. This panel is how residents communicate to the doorman and this particular button sends a silent alarm to the front desk, letting whoever is on duty know that police presence is required.

Assured that help is on the way, I slowly walk toward my father. My steps are hesitant, my body tense. I have no idea what he wants. Hell, he could just want to talk. But I'm not taking any chances.

"Why are you here?" I demand.

Dad opens the fridge and slams it shut again when he doesn't find what he's looking for. He whirls around to face me.

"Why am I here?" he repeats, and I nod.

He stomps forward, grabbing the lapels on my robe and pulling me toward him. My nose scrunches at his offensive odor, and I can't help but think about how far the mighty has fallen.

"Since when do I need a reason to visit my daughter?" he snarls.

I wrap my fingers around his wrists and attempt to push him away. His grip only tightens and the drunken rage on his face morphs into something I can't identify. Or don't *want* to identify.

His question is rhetorical, so I don't bother trying to answer. Even if he wanted a response, I'd be stupid to give one. I couldn't possibly give the right one.

Seemingly annoyed with my silence, Dad shoves me

12

away from him, and I stumble backward. I steady myself quickly and pull my robe tighter around me, as if the thin silk can protect me from whatever he might do.

"Here's the thing." Dad staggers back and forth, back and forth, unable to remain in a straight line. "I'm so close to the end. I just need a little more." He runs one hand through his thinning hair and sticks the other in his jacket pocket. "If I can do this, maybe things will go back to normal."

Unable to stay quiet any longer, I ask, "Do what?"

He stops in his tracks. "You're the only thing standing in my way."

I try to stay calm, but my nerves are tingling, reminding me that I'm anything but. Not that I needed the reminder. Anytime I'm around this man the woman I've become quickly falls away, leaving behind the scared little girl I used to be.

"How am I standing in your way?"

Dad removes his hand from his pocket, and metal flashes from between his fingers. A gun? I glance at it to get a better look, and my blood freezes in my veins. Not a gun, a knife. At least with a gun, whatever he's planning would be quick.

He closes the distance between us. My brain screams at me to move, but I can't get my feet to listen. He points the knife at my chest.

"You've always been in my way. If it weren't for you, I'd still be living a life of luxury."

And there it is, the real reason he's here.

"It's not my fault Mom left the money to me," I remind him. "Maybe if you hadn't been such a—"

Pain radiates through my jaw when his fist connects

with it and then through my hip as I fall and hit the side of the coffee table. The glass in the table shatters, and I can't stop the slivers that slice through my palms as I try to stand up, no more than I can stop the tears spilling down my cheeks.

"You always did talk too much," he sneers right before he kicks me in the stomach. Dad bends down to squat next to me. "I need that money, Fallon, and I'll get it... with or without your help."

He still reeks, but his words are no longer slurred. I can't help but wonder if he was as drunk as he seemed or if it was all an act. Not that it matters.

"Wh-what do you need it for?"

I have an idea, but I pray I'm wrong. Being right will complicate things in a way I'm not sure I can handle.

"It doesn't matter what I need it for."

I think back over everything he's said since barging through the door. None of it made sense and no matter how hard I—

I whip my head to look him in the eyes. They're black, cold, vacant. "You said you're almost to the end. The end of what?"

The intercom system buzzes before he has a chance to answer. You've gotta be kidding me. Now the doorman calls to get my permission to send someone up. What's the point of the fucking silent emergency button if this is how they're going to handle things?

"What's that?" Dad asks, raising his eyes to the door for a moment before returning them to my face. He presses the tip of the blade into my shoulder. "What did you do?"

I frantically shake my head. "I didn't do anything. I don't know what you're tal—"

"Stop!" he shouts, spittle flying from his lips and hitting me in the face. "How could you do this to me? The cops? Really?"

"Dad, I didn't call them," I insist.

It's not a lie. I didn't call them. I hit a goddamn button.

His face contorts, and the unfiltered rage I see flash in his expression scares me more than the knife.

"Miss Fallon." The doorman's voice comes through the intercom. "Miss Fallon, is everything alright?"

No, everything is not alright!

Even if I wanted to respond, I couldn't. You have to depress the button to do that. I refocus on my dad, on the sting of the knife digging into my flesh.

"You won't get away with this," I tell him, no longer caring if I instigate him further. If this is what is in store for me for the rest of my life, what's the point? I try to get help, and nothing ever happens. I can't live like this. "Do whatever it is you have to do to me but know that someone will come looking for you. You'll go to prison for the rest of your life and then what? Huh? You certainly won't get to the end of whatever the hell your game is from prison."

Without warning, he raises the hand holding the knife and plunges it into my side. Agony like I've never felt before tears through me. I've been beaten by this man more times than I care to remember, but this? This is new.

I open my mouth to speak but no words come out. All that I can manage is screams, and even those aren't coming out right.

My father, the one man who is supposed to love and protect me, continues to stab me, over and over again until I'm on the brink of passing out. Whether from pain or blood loss, I don't know.

The faint sound of banging reaches my ears, and I dig deep for the strength to stay conscious.

"Police!" A man shouts. "Open up!"

Again, I try to call out, but the only sound I can make is gurgled screams. I force my attention on my father, who has stopped stabbing me. He's standing up now, his head whipping in every direction, as if looking for a way out. He focuses on the window that leads to the fire escape.

Before he makes a run for it, he glares down at me and smirks. "We're not done here."

He draws his leg back, and just as he kicks me in the head, the door crashes open. Dad flees and gunshots ring out. I hear footsteps as several officers chase him out the window, but I know it'll be in vain. They won't catch him. And even if they do, he'll walk away a free man, just like always.

"Ma'am?" Another officer kneels next to me and talks into a two-way radio. When he's done, he grabs blankets from the couch and tries to keep pressure on my wounds. The problem is, there are too many. "Hang in there. The ambulance is on the way."

"I..." I twist to the side and spit up blood.

"Do you know who did this to you?" the officer asks. "Who was that running from the scene?"

"My..." I shake my head.

The events of the night are starting to fog in my brain. The more blood I lose, the more my memory fails. My head lulls to the side, and the officer smacks my cheek in an attempt to keep me awake.

"C'mon, stay with me," he pleads.

"M...my..." I start to shiver as my body goes numb. "C-call..." I try to swallow and immediately regret it when a thick metallic taste sticks in my throat. "Da..."

I slip over the edge and fall into an inky black hole. I hear the faint call of my name, and it echoes around me until it eventually disappears. The world as I know it is gone. I'm in this hole, and I have zero hope of ever coming back out.

CHAPTER 2
TOGA

The sound of my alarm buzzing pulls me from a deep sleep. Or more like a drunken coma. Last night's party was one for the books, and I drank way too much bourbon to even consider functioning today. I roll over and slap a hand over the button to shut the alarm off and kick free of the sheets. At least I'm waking up alone.

Lucky for me, the only thing on my agenda is my normal morning scour of the internet and a quiet day at home. There's no club business to handle, no rides to go on, no people to handle... nothing. This doesn't happen often, so when it does, I soak up every second.

I make my way to the bathroom, stumbling a bit as I do. Jesus, just how much *did* I drink? When I flip on the light, something on the mirror catches my attention. Scrawled in bright red lipstick are the words 'call me' and a phone number is under it.

Yeah right. I don't even know who you are.

Whoever was here last night, I'm grateful they left. I'm no stranger to one-night stands, but typically I have to be an asshole and kick the chick out in the morning.

I open the medicine cabinet and grab a bottle to dump a few Tylenol into my palm. I toss them in my mouth and then turn on the faucet and cup some water into my hands to wash them down. Hopefully they kick in quickly and dull my roaring headache.

Wanting to get to my computer, I take a shower in under five minutes. I wrap a towel around my waist and walk out to the kitchen to make some coffee. Once it's brewed, I pour a cup and carry it back into my bedroom so I can throw some sweats on and get to work.

I sit down on the mattress and pull my laptop from my nightstand. It takes a second for it to connect to the internet, but all the tabs in my browser from yesterday morning load. I start with news reports on the east coast.

There hasn't been activity there in several years, not since my mom divorced Ben, but I haven't been able to bring myself to stop checking. As far as I know, my mom still lives in the same town as when I left, despite everything Ben did to drive her away. As long as she's there, the east coast will still be on my radar.

News stories are depressing as hell, so I switch to social media. I bring up all the platforms I know Fallon's got a profile on. My eyes fixate on the picture she chose to use and no matter how hard I try, I can't pull my gaze from hers. It's crazy, really, because it's not her, not in the flesh, but it feels like she's staring right at me. It feels like she's reaching into my soul and digging her claws into all of my regrets, all of my shoulda, coulda, wouldas.

I shake the thoughts away and refocus on the task at hand: make sure Fallon is still doing okay and that her father hasn't caught up to her. Once I assure myself of those two things, I can go about my day and put it, and her, out of my mind until tomorrow morning when I repeat the process all over again. Same as I have for the last eight years, ever since the day I drove away from her, my mom, my life.

Scrolling through social media, I see Fallon is still preparing to open Source of Love. I've followed her journey and pride floods my system at how far she's come. From a scared teenager who thought she knew what she wanted to a woman with purpose and passion for making a difference. She's incredible. And as much as I love reading about her accomplishments and looking at her pictures, I wish I could tell her this in person. Even though she was only in my life for three and a half years, I've missed her more than anything else I walked away from.

I make a note that it's been almost twenty-four hours since Fallon posted anything on social media but force myself not to worry. She typically posts three or four times a day, especially on the page for the non-profit she set up, but it is the weekend. While it's unusual for her, it's not unheard of for people to take time to unplug.

Switching to the news in her area, I scroll through the police blotters and come up empty. Just the typical home invasions, assaults, and drunk drivers. Next, I look at the headlines. I'm about to wrap things up when one headline stands out.

Young Woman Stabbed and Left for Dead

The photo I was lost in moments ago mocks me from the screen.

"Fallon," I whisper on a shaky breath.

And next to it, is another photo of her, lying in a hospital bed, hooked up to machines and tubes, clinging to life. Once the shock wears off, anger surges through me. At this moment, my gut is telling me my life is about to change forever.

I skim through the article and phrases like 'unknown assailant', 'robbery gone wrong', and 'inefficient security protocols' jump out at me. My hands ball into fists as I continue reading.

When I get toward the end, I focus on the statement from the responding officer at the scene. He recalls bits and pieces of what transpired from the second they reached the building until Fallon was taken away by ambulance. He also states that her last words before losing consciousness were something along the lines of 'Call Da-' and he's not sure if she was trying to say 'Dad' or someone's name.

David. She was trying to say David. She'd never ask for her dad.

He then goes on to request the help of the public, asking anyone with information to contact the police. The officer provides the number for a tip-line and that's it. He knows as well as I do, that the tip-line likely won't give them shit. But he has to keep up appearances.

I slam the laptop shut, knowing what I have to do. I unplug my cell phone from the charger and dial my president's number.

"Hello," a feminine voice answers.

"Sami, I need Snow. Now," I demand. Sami is Snow's ol' lady, and I love her like a sister, but I don't have time to talk to her right now.

"This better be good," Snow grumbles when he comes on the line. "It's early and a rare day off."

"I'll make it quick then," I assure him. "I need some time off. I've got a few things I need to take care of in Cali."

A rustling sound comes through the line, and I imagine

it's Snow sitting up in bed. That's where I'd be if I had a woman like Sami next to me.

"Toga, what's going on?"

"I've got shit to do," I snap.

"Watch it," Snow barks. "I'm the last person you want to get a fucking attitude with."

I shove a hand through my hair and try to take a few deep breaths. It's almost impossible because of the rage continuing to build.

"Sorry, Prez," I mumble. "But I need this. It's nothing to do with the club, I assure you. And nothing that will bring trouble to our door. I just need to help a friend."

"I'm gonna need more than that, Toga, and you know it."

"I don't know what more to tell you. A friend of mine from my life before Satan's Legacy was almost killed last night. She's in the hospital, and I need to go to her."

"Her?"

I heave a sigh. "Yes, her."

The beat of silence that follows is deafening, but Snow finally speaks. "Fine. But you're not going alone."

"I don't need a fucking babysitter!"

"Never said you did. But when was the last time we helped someone out and it didn't blow back on the club?" He inhales but doesn't give me a chance to answer. "Never, that's when. I don't care where you go or what you do, but you're taking a brother with you. You're clearly not thinking with your head, and emotions can get a man killed."

"This has nothing to do with emotions," I protest. "She's a friend, and I want to make sure she's okay, that's it."

"Which could be accomplished with phone calls to the hospital."

"What the fuck, man? I'm the goddamn Sergeant at Arms. I can handle myself and anything that might come from it."

"Yeah, you are. And I'm sure you can. But it's not a chance I'm willing to take, especially when you're not giving me all the facts." I start to argue, but he cuts me off. "Save it, Toga. Either you take someone with you or I won't approve the time off. Those are your options. Which is it going to be?"

Recognizing the corner he's put me in, I concede. "Fine. But can I at least choose who I take?"

"Absolutely," Snow responds quickly and chuckles. "I'm not that big of a control freak."

Right now, yeah, you are.

In an effort to keep the peace, I thank him and end the call. As much as it pisses me off, Snow isn't wrong. Having a second person with me could prove useful. And maybe, just maybe, they'll also help me keep my emotions in check.

I dial another number and listen to it ring. When the call is answered, I don't even wait for a greeting.

"Magic, you up for a road trip?"

CHAPTER 3
FALLON

Images filter through the black hole I've been trapped in. I've been hearing sounds for a while, but I assumed it was all part of the process. It made sense to me. Getting into heaven can't be easy. And why wouldn't they screen newcomers? I made peace with it, but now? Now I don't know what to think. Is the process over? Was I finally approved for entry?

"Any change, Doc?"

David. I've heard his voice many times since dying. It makes me sad that he's here too, but it's not shocking. The last time I saw him he was riding away from his life like a bat out of hell. He probably got into an accident on that hunk of metal and is part of my heavenly welcoming committee.

"As you can see here, Fallon's brain waves are showing a little more activity. With each passing day, there's improvement."

Improvement? Last I checked, zombies weren't real, so how the hell can they improve on death?

"If that's true, why isn't she waking up?"

I recognize that voice too, but not because I know who it belongs to. It started squawking the same time David's did.

"It could be a number of things. The swelling has gone down, and the bleeding has stopped, so I'm betting her brain is trying to protect her. If she wakes up, she's likely to remember what happened. And the brain doesn't want that. It sounds hokey, but the brain is a funny thing."

I remember what happened. Every second of it. So your theory is bunk, Doc.

"I'll leave you two alone with her for a while. The nurse will be in to check on her, but other than that, you should have some privacy."

"Thanks, Doc."

The sound of a door shutting is like a shock to my system. Is this it? Are they going to welcome me in now?

"Her bruises are almost healed."

"Yeah."

"And the knife wounds they stitched up look good."

"Uh huh."

"Toga, c'mon, man," the other male voice pleads. "You've gotta snap out of it. If the doctor's right, she's going to wake up. And when she does, the last thing she needs is to see your mopey face."

Wait, who's Toga? I thought David was here.

"Fuck, Magic." That's definitely David's voice. "Who would do this?"

"You know who. Or at least, that's what you've been saying for the last two weeks."

Two weeks?! I've been like this for two fucking weeks? Wait, have I had this all wrong? Am I alive? I have to be because their conversation makes no sense otherwise.

David! Can you hear me?

"Knowing it and proving it are two different things, M."

"Maybe, but that's if you're operating under the confines of the law. We don't."

Huh?

"I'm not dragging the club into this, and I'm sure as hell not dragging her into anything illegal."

"You don't have to drag her into it. But if I had to guess, she's going to be in it whether you like it or not."

In what?

"Look, Toga, we can always go home and let the police do their thing. But you've already made it perfectly clear that her dad won't be punished for this. That's where we come in."

"I know, but..."

"But what, bro?"

David, or Toga, or whatever his name is, sighs.

"She can't get hurt again. I can't let that happen."

"And she won't. We'll take her to the club with us and plan. We'll take our time and do this right."

I'm not going anywhere with you! You left me, remember?

"She won't go."

"Of course she will," the man called Magic says. "She'd be stupid not to."

"Maybe, but she's not going to walk away from her life. Not with me anyway."

Damn straight.

"Fallon isn't like other women. She's strong, smart, and very passionate about the non-profit she's starting. She won't leave that behind."

He knows about that? How?

"Then make her, Toga. C'mon, I've seen you charm your fair share of chicks. Just do that to her."

"Ha! Yeah, right. Trust me, Magic, when she wakes up, you'll see just how impossible that is. You have no idea what you're talking about when it comes to Fallon."

"And you do?" Magic counters. "By your own admission, you haven't seen her in eight years. People change."

"She didn't. Other than becoming stronger, she's the same girl I knew. Driven, determined, stubborn."

"I'd say she's probably pretty fucking hot too."

"Don't," David growls. "She's off limits."

Uh, not your call.

A chair shuffles and footsteps sound around me.

"I'm gonna go get some coffee, kid." David's close. I can smell him, and if my brain would quit playing savior, I could probably touch him. "Magic will stay with you."

Footsteps sound again and then the door. The tension in the void surrounding me dissipates. I try like hell to get my eyes to open, my limbs to move. I need to do something, anything to make them realize I'm still in here.

"Fallon, I don't know if you can hear me, but our boy is on the edge here." A hand lifts mine. "I need you to wake up for him."

I'm trying!

My hand is dropped, and it sounds like Magic is pacing. "He's told me a lot about you in the last two weeks. More about your father though. Jesus, that guy's a piece of work, isn't he? I don't know how you survived him all these years."

Wake up, Fallon. Just open your eyes and say something. Wake. The. Fuck. Up.

"Toga's mentioned you over the years, but only in passing. He likes to think his morning routine is a secret, but it's not. We all know what he does on his laptop. Snow got suspicious because Toga was late to Church one day and had our tech guy dig a bit. We know more than he thinks, but he's determined to keep you to himself. Why is that? What happened between the two of you?"

So much, yet not nearly enough.

Somehow, I manage to get my fingers to wiggle a bit. Or at least I think I do. And if I can do that, I can open my eyes. C'mon, one at a time.

"I hope he's wrong about you. I hope you'll see reason and come to the club with us. We're a rowdy bunch, but we'll grow on ya. And you'll be safe. I don't know that the same will be true if you stay here. Your dad has a lot of clout, even if he's fallen far off his pedestal the last few years."

Open your—

There! Light. It's working. My vision is blurry through my right eye, but I convince myself if I can just get the left open, it'll clear. Machines beep around me, and I make out the silhouette of a man striding toward me.

"Fallon?" He leans over my face. "Oh my God, you're awake."

Fear slams into me, but I force it aside. David trusted this man, so he probably won't hurt me.

Do you want to pin your life on 'probably'?

"I..." My throat is dry, and my voice is scratchy. Rather than continue, I point to the water bottle I spot in his hand.

"Oh, yeah." He twists off the cap and holds it to my lips. I drink deeply, almost draining the liquid, in hopes it'll relieve some of the scratchiness. "Better?" he asks as he dabs the corner of my mouth.

I nod. "Thanks," I croak out.

"No problem."

"Magic, right?"

The man narrows his eyes at me. "How'd you know?"

"I've been listening."

"Oh."

"And I hate to break it to you, but..."

"But what?"

"David isn't wrong about me."

CHAPTER 4

TOGA

"Sir? Excuse me, sir."

The words barely register.

"Sir, you're holding up the line."

I lift my head and see that the cashier is right. I *am* holding up the line.

"Sorry."

I take a few steps forward and pay for the two coffees. One for me and one for Magic. As much as I wanted to do this all alone, there's no denying that he's been right there, every step of the way, and he hasn't judged me once. We might not always agree on everything, but if ever there's a brother I can trust with this, it's Magic. He's the one who brought me into the fold eight years ago, after all.

He might not know everything about my past, but he knows more than the others.

I make my way through the hospital, back toward Fallon's room on the eighth floor, and a flood of memories crashes through my mind.

The day Fallon and I met. The bruises on her arms she tried to hide. The turtleneck she was wearing even though it was a warm spring day. Her absolute dedication to school and bettering herself so she could get away from her father on her own and for good.

Fallon in the window as I rode away, and the long trip cross-country that ensued.

Meeting Magic after breaking up a fight. Apparently, I stepped into the middle of some shit I had no business seeing, but instead of taking out the witness, Magic invited me into the fold, asked me if I'd want to prospect for a club called Satan's Legacy.

I jumped at the chance at a home, a family, anything to call my own.

The elevator doors slide open, and I blink myself back into the present. I don't remember getting on the elevator or pressing any buttons. I stride down the hallway toward Fallon's room, and the closer I get, the louder the voices get.

I rush to the doorway and almost drop the coffees when I see Magic and Fallon arguing. Relief at seeing her awake is swift, but it's replaced by the instinct to protect her from my brother. I know he'd never hurt her, but apparently, yelling at Fallon is as off limits as commenting on her looks.

I rush to set the drinks down and grab Magic by his cut, forcing him back against the wall as I do.

"What the fuck do you think you're doing?" I snarl.

The hairs on the back of my neck stand on end, Fallon's stare penetrating through the haze I'm in. I can't see her, but I know she's watching, questioning, judging.

Magic wraps his hands around my wrists and pries them away from him. His face is set in stone, his eyes blazing.

"That's your one free pass, Toga," he sneers. "I hope it was worth it because the next time you put your hands on me, you won't be getting them back."

I shove a shaky hand through my hair and heave a sigh. This is not what I wanted Fallon's first impression of me to be after so many years.

"David?"

I whip my head around and lock eyes with her. Hers are wide, and she has her arms crossed over her chest as if to protect herself. There's a hint of fear emanating from her, but there's also a sense of determination.

Stealing myself against whatever emotions are rolling off her, I turn to face her fully and close the distance between me and the bed she's lying in. When I'm close enough to touch her, it takes all my willpower not to.

"Hey, kid." My voice is scratchy, almost as if emotion clogs my throat, but it can't be. I won't let it.

"I'm not going with you to..." She shifts her eyes to Magic and then back to me. "I'm not going with you."

"I've heard that before," I mumble.

"Yeah, you have," she agrees. "And you'll continue to hear it as long as there's breath in my body. I didn't need you then, and I don't need you now."

I let my gaze travel the length of her body, wishing I could see each and every bruise or stab wound and, at the same time, grateful I can't. The only thing seeing them would gain me is something to point out to her all the reasons why coming back to Colorado with me is her best chance at safety.

"If you'd just hear me out, I think you'd—"

"Hear you out?" Fallon tries to sit up but can't. She does her best to hide the pain that flickers on her face, but I see it. I see everything. "I think you need to hear *me* out for a change. I'm not running away to lick my wounds. I'm not leaving my life behind. I'm fine right here... without you."

Frustration boils just under the surface. She's being

irrational. And stupid. As long as she's alive, or her father is alive, she's in danger. It's as simple, and as complicated, as that.

Machines begin to beep as Fallon's heart rate climbs. The longer we stare at each other, the more upset she gets. And while I need her to see reason, I refuse to push her at the expense of her health.

"Uh, Toga," Magic begins from the opposite side of the room. "Maybe we should go, let her rest for a bit."

"I'm not fucking going anywhere."

"Yes, you are."

I lift my eyes toward the sound of the voice and see the doctor standing there, concern etched on his face. I open my mouth to tell him to go to Hell, but he holds up a hand before any words come out.

"I'm not banning you from the hospital, only requesting that you leave for a while to give Miss Hart a chance to calm down and get some rest." To his credit, the doctor is doing the best he can to allow us to stay. "The nurses need to check a few things anyway, so it's a good time to go get some coffee, or better yet, go home, take a shower, take a nap... whatever it is you need to do to calm down. And then you can come back."

"No, they can't," Fallon argues.

"Listen, Miss Hart, you're my patient and I'll honor your wishes, but it's not going to be easy to kick these two out. Trust me, I've tried. But they've been here since the day after you were brought in, and they haven't left your side. If you ask me, these are the people you want in your corner."

"I don't need anyone in my corner. I can handle myself."

"And your injuries say otherwise," the doctor counters before looking at me. "Please, go. You can come back in a few hours."

I weigh the options in my mind. I could certainly push the issue, and Magic and I could stay. It wouldn't be too hard to do. Or I could listen to the doc and give Fallon a little time. I'm not crazy about either, but I know the second option will be far less damaging to Fallon and her opinion of me.

"Fine." I nod and look at Fallon. "We'll be back in a few hours, kid."

"I really wish you wouldn't be."

"Yeah, I know. But we don't always get what we want, now do we?"

CHAPTER 5
FALLON

"They should be here any minute."

I roll my eyes at the nurse, same as I have for the last five days. She clearly has a thing for both David—no, Toga—and Magic, as evidenced by the way she practically swoons every time they walk into my hospital room.

"I don't want them here," I say, not that it will do me any good. It hasn't so far.

"But honey, why?" The nurse hands me a pair of scrubs to change into. "They're every woman's fantasy and you could have either of them."

I stand from the bed and stretch, wincing at the pain. After walking into the bathroom, I shut the door on the nurse and her babbling about what she'd do to them if she had the chance. Once upon a time I'd have agreed with her where Toga is concerned, but not anymore.

He's still sex on a stick and you know it.

Staring at myself in the mirror, I untie the hospital gown and let it fall to the floor. Toga may be hot as fire, but I'm certainly not. At least not right now. My bruises have healed, but I still have countless stab wounds and slashes on my torso. They're healing, but not fast enough. And let's not forget about the stitched-up gash on my head where my father kicked me. Everything about me screams ugly. Even if there weren't physical reminders of my father's attack, there are mental ones, and I'll only be able to hide those for so long.

I slowly push my arms through the sleeves of the shirt and tug it over my head, savoring the split second where my reflection is hidden from view. The pants are next, and by the time I'm fully dressed, I can hear the nurse talking to Toga and Magic in the room.

Opening the door, I stand there and take in the woman flirting with Toga. I watch as he rebuffs each of her advances, even winking at me a time or two while he does it. Annoyance washes over me, along with a sliver of jealousy, both of which are unwelcome.

"What are you doing here?" I finally ask, unable to stand the show any longer.

The nurse whips her head in my direction and there's no mistaking the gasp that passes her lips. Her wide eyes remind me of a child caught with their hand in the cookie jar. Magic suppresses a laugh and Toga smirks.

Damn them all!

"We're here to take you home," Toga says after erasing the smirk off his face.

"I already told you, I'm not going with you."

"And if you'd paid attention to a word I've said over the last few days, you'd know that I'm taking you home to your place, not mine."

"I pay atten—" I slam my mouth shut and lock eyes with Toga. "Wait. You're not taking me to Colorado?"

Toga smirks and shakes his head.

"And I'm going back to my place?"

"Sure are."

"Oh."

The reality of me being discharged from the hospital sets in, and now I don't know how to feel about going home. On one hand, I'm glad Toga finally listened and isn't forcing the issue of me leaving. I've got too much to do for my grand opening and already lost three weeks. On the other hand, how the hell am I supposed to walk back into my condo and not relive the attack, over and over again?

"Is something wrong?" Toga asks, pulling me from my quandary.

I shake my head and force my lips to lift. "No, of course not."

"Fallon, if you're scared, you don't have to go back to the condo. You can find another place or take us up on the offer of Colorado. No matter what you decide, I'll be there, which means you'll be safe."

I narrow my eyes at Toga. "What do you mean you'll be there?"

"Exactly that. If you think I'm going to just walk away and let you handle Ben on your own, you're crazy."

"That's not such a leap, David," I deadpan. "It's precisely what you did eight years ago."

"Okay, you two." Magic steps between us. "Can we not rehash this right now?" He glances toward the nurse who's still standing there, taking it all in. "You'll have plenty of time to argue after we get the hell out of here." He turns his head and focuses on Toga. "And we need to get the hell out of here if we want any chance of doing it alive. The paper has already hit the stands announcing her release from the hospital and we don't know who's seen it or what awaits us outside."

"Oh, right," the nurse finally pipes up. She hands me a stack of papers, as well as a plastic bag full of wound care items. "Here are your discharge instructions. The biggest thing is to make sure you keep all around the wound sites clean. The stitches that remain will fall out on their own, so you don't need to worry about that." She fidgets with her hands as she shifts her gaze to the men before returning it to me. "And the doctor would prefer it if you aren't alone for the first few days. You've been under constant monitoring and supervision here in the hospital. Not to mention under armed guard. If you're not comfortable with either of them being with you, call a friend."

Friend? I don't have many friends. I've got acquaintances, people I'll be working with and who have helped me with the non-profit, but as for someone I'd want in my home twenty-four-seven? Not so much.

"Don't worry," I assure her. "I'll be fine."

"Yes," Toga adds. "She will."

I roll my eyes at him. He's so full of himself. And he thinks he's staying with me. Newsflash... not happening. But I'll deal with that once I get home. For now, I need to focus my energy on getting out of the hospital because apparently, it's dangerous for me to leave.

"Well, good luck," the nurse says and exits the room.

"I thought she'd never leave," Magic huffs, but he doesn't take his eyes off the door.

"Yeah, right." Toga chuckles. "That's why you've been talking about banging her ever since we got here."

"Would you two shut up," I snap, pressing a hand to my forehead to stop the headache that's forming. I can feel their eyes on me, but I don't look at them. "Just get me outta here."

"Yes, ma'am," Magic says sarcastically.

Before I know it, I'm being wheeled down the hall to the elevator. I tried to insist that I didn't need the wheelchair, but according to the orderly, it's hospital policy. A small argument ensues when Toga hits the button for the basement. I tune the men out though and let them handle it. At this point, that's all I can do.

"We'll take her from here," Toga says when the doors slide open.

He wraps his hand around my arm and helps me stand up from the chair, not that I need it. It wasn't my legs that were affected by my attack.

"Sir, I really don't think that's a good idea," the orderly argues.

"And I really don't give a fuck what you think," Toga snaps. "She's been discharged and she's no longer the responsibility of this place. She's mine."

"Dude, I suggest you don't argue with him." Magic's words are directed at the now subtly shaking orderly. "It's his girl, and he's cranky from lack of food and sleep. And he's certainly in no mood to deal with your pitiful attempt to follow the rules."

The guy puts his hands up in mock surrender and opens his mouth to speak.

"Don't," Toga bites out. "Trust me when I say it's in your best interest to listen to what my brother here is saying."

The orderly steps back onto the elevator and stabs his finger at the button frantically until the doors close.

"Now that you've scared this shit out of some poor man just trying to do his job, how about you fill me the hell in about what's going on?" I rest my hands on my hips and ignore the flash of pain the movement causes.

"Fallon, you know as well as I do the media frenzy that

surrounds cases like this," Toga responds as he thrusts a hand through his longish hair.

"Cases like this?"

He tilts his head and gives me a look that might as well scream 'idiot'. "Yeah, you know… a young woman who's making a life for herself after escaping a nightmare childhood gets stabbed by an unknown assailant." Toga smirks. "Are there secrets in her closet or is this totally random? Those kinds of cases."

"I see."

But I really don't. Who gives a shit about a transplant from across the country? Certainly not the elite. I was never the one in the family the media followed around. That was reserved for the great Ben Hart, self-made billionaire who had a dark side no one knew about. Only he wasn't self-made. The image he created was done with the money my mother's family earned with their own sweat, blood, and tears.

Toga leads me through a maze of halls until we reach another elevator labeled 'employees only'. Magic follows close behind, almost as if he's waiting for someone to commit a sneak attack. We step onto the elevator and take it to the first floor. It opens up into what appears to be an abandoned hall but there are several cafeteria workers which tells me we're likely near some service entrance.

"This way," one of the workers says and urges us to follow him.

We do and just before we exit the building, Toga slaps money into the worker's palm and gives him a curt 'thanks'.

Once outside, I stop in my tracks, because parked only feet from the entrance is my car, along with a motorcycle. Toga tugs on me to walk around to the passenger side before he opens the door.

"Get in," he barks, constantly looking over his shoulder.

"I can drive," I protest and try to extricate myself from his grasp.

He gently shoves me down and into the vehicle before slamming the door. When he slides in the driver's seat, I glare at him.

"What was that for?" I demand.

Toga turns in his seat and locks eyes with me. "Look, kid. I know I'm not your favorite person. I know you want nothing to do with me. But you're shit out of luck because we both know Ben won't stop. I walked away once, and I'll be damned if I do it again." He draws in a big breath before blowing it out slowly, as if trying to calm his frustration. "So, you're going to sit there and shut up while I drive us to your place. And when we get there, you're going to say thank you to Magic for being here so he can leave. Then, and *only* then, will we sort through our shit so we can *hopefully* work out a plan." He pauses briefly. "Now, can you do that for me? Please?"

I stare at him a moment, soaking up the fire in his eyes, the way his jaw tics every few seconds. This man is the same man who rode away from me eight years ago and so much about him is the same: his hair color, the dimple in his cheek, the slight cleft in his chin, his attitude, his determination. Yet, there's so much that's different. And it's the different that has me uttering the one word that could get me into a mountain of trouble.

"Yes."

CHAPTER 6

TOGA

The drive to Fallon's apartment is tense. Silence engulfs me, making my insides itch and my mind wander. I know I told her to shut up and let me drive, but fuck, I didn't mean for it to be taken to this extreme.

When I pull into the parking garage and glide into her designated spot, Fallon makes no move to exit the car. Determination swirls with frustration in her eyes, no doubt waging war and causing her to fear what's next: getting out of the car and walking into what was a crime scene, *her* crime scene.

"We're home," I say, reaching out to touch her arm.

Fallon flinches and whips her head in my direction. I can't unsee the flicker of pain the motion causes, but I choose to ignore it... for now.

"This isn't your home."

Annoyance flares. "No shit. It's an expression."

I take a deep breath to keep myself from losing my composure, and the sound of Magic's Harley echoes in the structure. *That* sound, more than anything, is what does the trick. He pulls in next to my bike and cuts the engine. My body relaxes, but it doesn't last long.

"He can't park there," Fallon says. "I only pay for the one space."

Again, I breathe in, out, in, out. "Turns out there is a tenant on vacation. Your landlord is graciously allowing us to pay a hundred bucks a day to rent the parking space," I tell her sarcastically. "Fucking prick drove a hard bargain."

Fallon cracks a small smile but quickly hides it. "Oh."

I stare at her, this person who's a mixture of the girl I left and the woman she's become. She's picking at her already badly chipped nails just like she used to do as a teenager. Images of Fallon sitting on my bed, scraps of hot pink nail polish on her lap, flood my mind.

She's scared. Terrified to go inside and face the hell that awaits, the memories, the nightmare.

But she has you.

And she's resisting that as hard as she can.

Stop letting her.

The conversation with myself goes on and on as I continue to watch Fallon. I reach across the seat and lift one of her hands in mine, fully expecting her to pull away. She doesn't. Instead, her cold fingers wrap around my warm ones, and she squeezes... hard.

"It's going to be okay," I say quietly, afraid to spook her.

Fallon shakes her head, and a tear spills over her cheek. "No, it's not." She swipes at the salty evidence of her fear and pain with her free hand and then looks at me. The cracks in my heart splinter a little bit more. "It's never been okay, and it never will be."

It would be if she listened to me, came back to Colorado and let me protect her, let my club protect her. But I keep that to myself because instinctually, I know that saying it to her again, in this moment, would push her away even more. And that's the last thing I want.

"Why don't we go—"

A sharp knock on the passenger window startles Fallon and she jumps. I glare at Magic through the glass behind her.

"What the fuck, bro?" I snap.

Magic motions for me to roll the window down, but the car is off, so I can't. Instead, we continue to shout through the barrier.

"We need to get inside," Magic says with a sharp bite to his tone. "Something isn't right."

I swivel my head to take in our surroundings as much as I can from my position in Fallon's car. I don't see anyone or anything that looks suspicious. Problem is, I've learned to trust Magic's gut as much as my own.

"What's he talking about?" Fallon asks, her voice shaky. "What's wrong?"

"Nothing," I assure her, even though I'm guessing it's a lie. "But he's right. We should go inside, get you settled. It's been a long couple of weeks."

Fallon narrows her eyes, and I know she doesn't believe me, but she doesn't argue. She slips her hand from mine and robotically turns to reach for her bag in the backseat. I stop her, unwilling to sit by and watch her silently go through the motions.

I grab the bag and quickly step out of the car to circle it and help Fallon. Before I even get to the passenger's side, my eyes land on Magic, who's gingerly helping Fallon out of the car and guiding her toward me.

My blood boils and jealousy shoots through me like a pinball ricocheting with each strike of a bumper. I don't give a shit if Magic is my brother or that I know he wouldn't cross that line, or even that there really isn't a line to cross. No one, and I do mean *no one*, needs to be touching Fallon but me.

"Dude, what's wrong?" Magic asks as he drops his arms to his sides. Both of them focus on me.

I shake away the rush of unwanted emotions. "Not a damn thing."

Magic gives a knowing smirk, and I narrowly manage to resist the urge to beat the shit out of him. He knows exactly what he's doing and is enjoying every second. "Uh huh," he mumbles.

Fallon glances back and forth between us but, thankfully, doesn't ask any questions. I don't know what I'd say if she did.

"Let's get inside."

I close the distance between Fallon and me, wrapping my arm around her shoulders when I reach her. She tries to shrug free, but I maintain my hold because I'm doing this just as much for me as I am for her.

I lead Fallon through the parking garage, past her doorman, and into the elevator to take it up to her floor. The longer we walk, the closer she gets to me. I don't know if she even realizes she's doing it, nor do I care. At least I know there's a part of her that wants me here, whether she'll admit it or not.

Magic follows close behind. When we get to her door, I shove a hand into my pocket to grab the key but stop short when Fallon gasps. Her eyes grow wide, and I follow her gaze.

The door is cracked open the slightest bit. I quickly glance at Magic and see him already holding his gun and braced to enter. I follow suit.

"Fallon, stay here," I order her, pushing her against the wall next to the door.

She nods frantically, and I frown at her. I was expecting an argument, some part of her stubborn streak to show. The fact that it's nowhere to be seen saddens me. Ben really did a number of her and not just physically.

Magic and I enter the apartment, one after the other, and sweep the place. We clear every room, finding them empty. There's no evidence that someone was in here, other than the open door. Did Magic or I forget to close it completely when we left this morning? My gut tells me no. But everything in front of me tells me otherwise.

"Can I come in?"

I turn toward the door and see Fallon poking her head in. I shove my gun into the back of my waistband, as does Magic.

"Sure."

It takes a few moments, but Fallon finally enters. "Find anything?"

I shake my head. "We must not have shut the door all the way when we left."

"Pretty stupid mistake if you're as worried about my safety as you say you are," she counters.

Before I can respond, Magic does. "Maybe. But we're human."

I can tell by the tone of his voice that he doesn't believe we did anything wrong any more than I do. I don't know if that's good or bad.

Fallon walks across the room, toward her kitchen, but stops short of crossing where she was found by police. The blood stains have been cleaned and there is nothing physical to remind her of what happened, but mentally? She'll never forget.

I walk to her and rest my hand on the small of her back. "You're safe," I remind her. "We're not going to let anything happen to you. *I'm* not going to let anything happen to you."

"So you keep saying."

"Yeah, I do. Because it's the truth." I urge Fallon to face me fully and lock eyes with her. "You're safe with me. No matter what happens or how much you hate me, I promise I'll keep you safe."

Fallon appears to think about that for a moment before nodding. Then she extricates herself from my hold and disappears into her bedroom, leaving me alone with Magic.

"You sure that's a promise you can keep, Toga?"

I glance at him, my face stone cold.

"I don't have a choice."

CHAPTER 7
FALLON

My eyes dart around my bedroom as I enter it. I can't shake the uneasy feeling in the pit of my stomach, despite Toga and Magic clearing my entire apartment. At the hospital, it was easy to keep my walls up and feel confident that I could come home and be okay on my own. Now that I'm at my apartment, at the damn crime scene where I almost died, I'm grateful Toga is here. Not that I'd admit that to him.

I walk to my closet to find clothes to change into, something more comfortable, and my eyes land on my robe. No, not my robe... a robe. I was wearing mine the night my father came. And based on my injuries, it had to have been ruined.

Toga must have replaced it.

Wrapping my hands in the floral silk material, I bring it to my face and savor the luxurious feel. The kimono style and NOIRI tag gives me some indication about what he paid for the robe, and I can't help but wonder why. To win me over? Or are his intentions simpler and asshole-ish?

Right now, I really don't care. I just want this expensive

48

garment against my skin. I undress before pulling the robe from the hook next to the closet and slipping it on. It fits perfectly, falling to mid-thigh and accentuating my curves in a sexy, yet comfortable way. I don't bother tying the silk sash, instead choosing to leave my body exposed.

Next, I go into my bathroom, needing to get a look at myself, to assess my injuries in a better light than the hospital. Surely, they aren't as bad as they looked there. I lock the door behind me and step in front of the mirror. But I don't look, not yet.

Air gets trapped in my lungs as I try to breathe. I've never considered myself to be vain but standing here with my eyes squeezed shut and my knees threatening to buckle, I realize I just might be. Or maybe I'm just scared as hell to see the permanent damage my father did. And *that* is more than unbearable.

A knock startles me enough that in a split second I find my eyes open staring at my reflection. With my robe open, nothing is hidden from my view and it's as if I'm being attacked all over again.

"Fallon," Toga calls through the door. "Everything okay?"

I nod. Emotion clogs my throat making it impossible to speak. I swipe at the tears running down my cheeks as I keep trying to get myself under control.

The doorknob jiggles. "Fallon?"

I swallow past the lump and catch my breath. "I-I'm fine."

The jiggling continues. "C'mon, Kid. I can hear you crying. You're not fine."

Part of me wants to curl up in a ball and disappear, never let anyone see me again. The other part of me, the bigger part of me, wants to open the door and let Toga in. If I can stand his scrutiny, I can stand anyone's.

I reach for the lock and twist it so he can enter. It doesn't take him but a fraction of a second to push open the door and step beside me. The bathroom shrinks around me as his large frame fills the space.

Averting my eyes, I stare at the counter to avoid meeting his gaze in the mirror. Toga rests his hand on my shoulder, gently at first, but the longer we stand there in silence, the tighter his grip becomes. I pull my robe closed.

"I'm gonna fucking kill him," he snarls.

Without thinking about my actions, I reach up and lay my hand over his. His fingers immediately unclench, and he pulls away from me.

"Sorry." Toga crosses his arms over his chest, almost as if he's trying to keep himself from reaching out again. "I didn't mean to hurt you."

"I know."

Toga begins to pace. My bathroom is larger than most, but it feels way too small with him in it and angry. He reminds me of a bull in a china shop.

"How could he do this to you?" he asks, although it seems more a rhetorical question than anything. "Sure, you're an adult, but you're still his child. I don't get it. I mean, I'd never lay a goddamn hand on Lennox or Shiloh, or any other kid for that matter."

My stomach bottoms out at the mention of children. His children. There was a time I fancied myself in love with him and pictured us with two point five kids, a dog, and a white picket fence. Those foolish dreams are long gone, or so I thought.

I take a deep breath and force words out of my mouth. "How old are they?"

Toga stops pacing and faces me. "Who?"

"Lennox and Shiloh, your kids."

His eyes widen for a moment before he bursts into laughter. Annoyance winds through me. It's a logical question, and I fail to see the humor.

"Damn, Fallon," he says when he finally sobers. "That's funny. Never knew you were a comedian." He must notice my frustration because his expression turns serious. "I don't have kids. Lennox is Sami's son and Snow's soon to be stepson, and Shiloh is Laney's son and Snow's nephew. I'd do anything for them as if they were my own, but they aren't."

"Oh." There's nothing else to say. I've managed to make an ass out of myself and rather than being frustrated, or even jealous, I'm embarrassed. I'd take most other emotions any day over that.

Toga closes the distance between us but stops short of touching me. "We've covered kids, but for the record, no wife, no girlfriend, no one special."

Before I can comment, Magic's voice comes through the door.

"Bro, you about done in there? I gotta head out."

Toga pulls his cell from his pocket and glances at it. "Dude, you've got a few hours."

"Snow just called and ordered me back. I don't have a choice, man."

Magic's tone bleeds worry. I've heard it from him before, but not like this. Something is really wrong.

Toga yanks the door open. "What's going on?" he demands. "What about what we've got going on here?"

"I think you can handle..." Magic's gaze darts to me for a moment. "... this. You know the enemy, Toga."

"That's not the point," Toga counters. "We were both

cleared to be here. Whatever the fuck is going on back home, they can deal without us, and you know it."

"Well, for some reason, Snow doesn't seem to think so."

Toga's muscles tense, and he steps toward Magic. I can see the anger in him building in the way his face reddens, his fists clench, his entire demeanor sparks like a stick of dynamite being lit. I step between the two with no other thought in mind than to diffuse the situation.

I glance from Toga to Magic and back again. "Maybe you should go with him?" Toga's eyes narrow, and I shrug. "What? They're your family, right?"

The question burns. There was a time when I was his family, or at least part of it. And as angry as I've been with him through the years, as much hatred that I've held in my heart for him, I'd be lying if I said I didn't wish we had some connection now.

He came when you were hurt.

That's true. But did he come for me or did he come for revenge? Because those are two very different things.

"Yeah, they're family," Toga confirms with a huff. "But so are you."

I have nothing to say to that. In a split second, my wish is coming true, and at the same time, I don't trust it. After what feels like hours of silence, I let out a chuckle.

"In another life, maybe. But right now?" I shake my head. "We're not family. Not anymore."

Before Toga can respond, Magic rests a hand on my shoulder. "I hate to break it to you, Darlin', but you are family. To Toga, to me, and to the rest of Satan's Legacy. The second Toga made the decision to be here because you needed him, you became family."

Um, what?!

"I didn't need him," I argue. "I still don't nee—"

"Give it up, Fallon." Magic drops his hand and turns toward the door. "You need him just as much as he needs you. Someday, you'll figure that out. I just hope it's before Ben gets the drop on you."

Magic disappears from the bathroom doorway and out of my bedroom. The creak of the front door opening pulls both Toga and I from our stupor and we rush to follow Magic.

"Figure this shit out, Toga," Magic calls over his shoulder. "In the meantime, call if you need anything."

The door closes, and just like that, Magic is gone. Toga and I are alone. I'm left to try and follow my thoughts as they spin out of control.

Now what?

What were Toga's motives for coming here?

And how does me being attacked make me family?

And more importantly, how the hell do I feel about that?

CHAPTER 8
TOGA

"You're not going."

Fallon has said the same thing five times, and she can say it fifty more. She's not leaving this apartment without me.

"I thought you had a meeting to get to," I remind her.

"I do."

I glance at my phone to check the time. "Then I suggest you quit arguing with me because you're already late."

Fallon lifts her cell to look at the screen and groans. "When are you going home?" she asks me.

"Not before your meeting."

Pulling open the door, I gesture for her to go into the hall. She stands her ground for a moment and then caves. We've played this same song and dance for two days now, and I can't help but wonder when it's going to change, when she's going to stop fighting the fact that I'm here and I'm not going anywhere.

The silence that ensues once we get on the elevator is deafening. And by the time we get to her car, I worry that my ear drums will shatter.

"Remind me again what this meeting is about."

Fallon startles at my instruction but quickly recovers. She fidgets with her hands, her nervous energy overpowering her annoyance with my presence.

"It's with my accountant," she responds. "Just to finalize a few things. Then, this afternoon, I meet with the Board of Directors to finalize staffing."

"Sounds important."

"It is." Fallon turns to look at me from the passenger seat. "So don't fuck it up."

My grip on the steering wheel tightens. "How the hell would I fuck it up?"

"I don't know," she admits. "Just by being there, maybe. Or by opening your mouth and voicing your opinion. There are lots of ways."

"Your faith in me is overwhelming," I drawl.

"My faith in you is based on history. It's based on the fact that you came here and are trying to take over my life. My faith in you, or lack thereof, is on you." She swivels to look out her window. "Take responsibility for your actions, Toga, and quit trying to lay blame where it doesn't belong."

My insides churn, twisting into a knot of anger. I wish I could say it was all directed at Fallon because then it would be an easier problem to solve. All I'd have to do is pack up and go home, leaving her to pick up the pieces. But my emotions are not her fault.

They're mine, and my actions are the reason she feels the way she does. I chose to leave eight years ago, to walk away and save myself. Ben chose to be a horrible parent and pitiful excuse for a human. My mother chose to marry Ben, to put her toxic relationship before me and anyone else around her. But Fallon? While she chose to stay and finish her education, she didn't choose anything else. Not her parents, her upbringing, my actions... none of it.

"Do you really have nothing to say?"

I glance at her out of the corner of my eye and huff out a breath before returning my focus to the road. We're almost to her office and the last thing I need is to miss my next turn and make her even more late.

"I have plenty to say, but now isn't the time."

"Since when has bad timing ever stopped you?"

"Fuck, Fallon, are you spoiling for a fight or what? Because I can give you one if you want, but I'd prefer to drop it until we're back to your place if it's all the same to you."

"Fine. But I think we've put off a few discussions long enough. We talk tonight or you leave."

"Works for me."

"Good."

I open my mouth to spit out some smart-ass comment but slam it shut before I can. This argument could drag on forever if we let it, and just because I have this need to get in the last word doesn't mean I should.

"Turn left at the next light."

"I know."

"Then you'll make a right at the third light after that."

"I know."

"My building will be on the left."

"I know."

"And there's a parking garage across the street. We don't have our sign up yet, but you can't miss the big 'lease' sign that's sti—"

"Fallon!" I snap.

"What?"

"I. Know."

"How?" She throws her hands in the air. "How could you possibly know all of—"

"I just do."

"But how?"

I let out a groan. "Do you really believe I'd come here to protect you and not do my homework? I made sure to know all I could about where you live, where you work, and that includes how the fuck to get there. Besides..." I make the right at the third light and clamp my mouth shut.

"Besides...?" she prompts.

"Nothing."

"Wow. Really?"

I roll my eyes, grateful she can't see that while I'm focused on the road. "I know more than you think, okay. Can we please leave it at that, for now?"

"Fine." She twists to grab her bag out of the backseat and places it in her lap. "But add it to the list of things we'll be discussing tonight."

As I pull into the parking garage, I notice her hand on the door, gripping the handle while she waits for me to park. Only, she doesn't wait... not really. Before I even come to a full stop in the empty spot, she opens her door. The second I hit the brakes, her feet hit the ground and she's walking away.

"You've gotta be kidding me," I mumble under my breath.

I throw the car in park and turn it off so I can follow her. Fallon definitely isn't making it easy for me to keep calm. Her recklessness and complete disregard for her own safety is hurdling me toward my MC mindset faster than I can blink.

"Fallon!" I call out to her as she makes her way down the steps. "Wait up!"

When I catch up to her, it takes all of my willpower not to grab onto her arm and spin her around to face me. I want to lash out, yell and make her see things from my perspective. Instead, I fall into step next to her, biding my time until our conversation tonight.

If Fallon thinks it's going to be an easy one, she has a rude awakening ahead of her. And even *I* don't likely know the half of it.

I've got the rest of the day to let my thoughts percolate, and I'm not sure if that's a good thing or not.

CHAPTER 9
FALLON

Stepping out of the shower, I inhale deeply. On the way home, we stopped at a grocery store, of Toga's choosing of course, and picked up the things needed for him to make dinner. I wasn't expecting anything fancy, but judging by the smells coming from my kitchen, I'm going to get something delicious.

There's a sharp knock on the door, followed by Toga's voice. "You almost done?"

"I'll be out in a minute."

"Okay. Dinner's ready, so I hope you're hungry."

As if on cue, my stomach growls. "I could eat."

His rumbling chuckle flows through the door, as do his retreating footsteps. I quickly dry off and pull on a pair of sweats. I don't bother blow drying my hair, but I do run a comb through it before tugging a long-sleeved tee over my head.

When I exit the bedroom, the smells intensify and my mouth waters. I enter the kitchen and stop in my tracks as Toga comes into view. He has his back to me and all he's wearing is a pair of red sweats which are draped low on his

59

hips. As he transfers food from pans to plates, his muscles ripple and my mouth waters for an entirely different reason.

Get a grip, Fallon. We don't like this man.

Liking a man and being immensely attracted to him aren't the same thing at all. One I can control. And the other? My hormones don't allow me any control.

"Have a seat," he says as he turns around to carry the plates to the table. "I hope you like Asian food."

I love it but no need to reveal that to him. "It's okay."

Toga pulls out a chair for me, but I don't sit. It's weird, him displaying manners. He's been bossy as hell since the moment I woke up in the hospital. Sure, he's had his moments where sweet trumped asshole, but those are few and far between and they certainly don't make up for eight years ago.

"C'mon, Fallon," he grumbles. "Would you just sit down?"

I step around him and take another chair. It's petty, childish, but I don't care.

Toga shakes his head. "Why do you have to make things so—"

His cell phone rings from his pocket, and he pulls it out to look at the screen before answering.

"Hey, Snow," he greets. "What's up, man?"

I can't hear both sides of the first few minutes of the conversation. Then Toga sets the phone on the table and hits the speaker button.

"Can you repeat that, Prez?" Toga asks. "I've got you on speaker with Fallon, and I think this is something she should hear."

"Sure thing," the man—Snow—agrees. "Hi Fallon, nice to meet you." He chuckles. "Sort of."

"Oh, um, you too."

"I don't know how much my boy, Toga, has told you, but you can trust me. You've got a lot of people in your corner now, ya hear me?"

I glance at Toga, and his lips tilt upward into a grin. I don't know if he finds this exchange funny or if he's just happy that someone else is telling me the same things he has. Either way, I want to smack the expression off his face.

"Honestly, sir, he hasn't told me much."

Toga's face falls. "Because you won't listen!"

"Or maybe you just haven't tried hard enough," I counter, enjoying his uncomfortable squirming.

"Jesus, Toga, have I taught you nothing about women?" Snow asks, breaking up the tension. "You may have a way with the fairer sex, but shit, you've still got a lot to learn. And I can see the first lesson needs to be in communication."

"Shut up."

"Now is that any way to talk to your president?"

I can tell from Snow's tone that he's having fun with this, with Toga. I don't know him well enough to determine if there's any level of truth to what he's saying, but I can only imagine. The Toga I used to know was a ladies' man who didn't have the first clue about women.

Before Toga can respond, Snow continues. "As for you, Fallon." My enjoyment of the moment disappears. "Please just call me Snow. Or Zeke. 'Sir' makes me feel old."

"I can do that Si... Snow."

"Good girl." A shuffling noise comes through the line, and Snow clears his throat. "As fun as this has been, I've got shit to do so let's get back on track."

"Yes, let's," I agree.

"Fallon, Toga asked one of the club members, Brady, to

do some digging and find out what he could about the investigation into your attack." Snow pauses and takes a deep breath. "Turns out, there isn't much of an investigation. The case hasn't been officially closed, but it doesn't seem there are any detectives actually doing any work on it."

Shock slams into me, and I shoot out of my chair to lean on the table. Bracing myself on my palms, I take a few deep breaths to calm myself before speaking. It doesn't work.

"What the fuck do you mean they aren't working the case?" I demand.

"Exactly that."

"That's impossible. I was almost killed," I cry. "He's going to get away with attempted murder."

"He won't get away with it," Toga snarls. "I promise you that."

"Toga's right." Snow clears his throat. "Brady's damn good at finding things that no one wants found. He managed to track down some emails between the police commissioner and an anonymous man, who we think is your father. In a nutshell, those emails detail payouts from Ben Hart to the commissioner for the investigation to be squashed."

"He has no money!" I shout. "I didn't give him any that night. He's broke so it isn't possible."

"He might be broke, but loan sharks aren't."

I rub my temples to try and stop the migraine that's forming. "I can't... This is..." I lift my head and lock eyes with Toga. "I'm never going to be safe, am I?"

There's a desperation in my voice, one I despise. I don't want to have to rely on this man and his band of misfits, but I may not have a choice.

"Yes, Fallon, you will be safe." Toga rounds the table

and wraps an arm around my shoulders to pull me into his side. "You just might have to compromise a little on how we make that happen."

Without thinking, I bury my face in Toga's bare chest. His skin is warm, and his scent is comforting. It reminds me of a time when things between the two of us were good, normal.

"Anything else, Snow?"

There's an audible hesitation, a sharp breath that comes through the line. There's more that he has to say, and he doesn't want to say it. Whether it's because I can still hear or because it's just not something positive, I have no idea.

"We've got some shit going down here, a few members who need an attitude adjustment. As the Sergeant at Arms, that's your job. So far, we're handling it and the guys are having fun, but..."

Toga stiffens and his arm tightens around me. "But what?"

"I'm gonna need your ass back here soon."

"How soon?"

"You've got a few more days, but that's it. We need you."

I tilt my head to look at Toga, and his face is scrunched up in what can only be described as frustration. He runs his free hand through his short mohawk, mussing it up.

"Fine," he finally says. "I'll figure something out."

A woman's voice comes through the line, but it's distant.

"I better let you go so you can take care of that." Toga's tension dissipates a little and he chuckles.

"*That* is going to be the death of me. Lennox has been

63

with my sister all day, and Sami has been taking advantage of privacy... but I'm not complaining."

"I'm sure you're not. Go take care of your ol' lady, Prez. I'll check in later."

"Be sure you do."

With that, Snow ends the call. Toga picks up his phone and shoves it into his sweat's pocket and then twists to face me, so I'm forced to take a step back. Immediately, I miss his body heat, his scent... him.

When he rests his hands on my shoulders, he bends slightly to be at eye level.

"We should probably have that conversation now."

CHAPTER 10
TOGA

Dinner is quiet. Somber. I've opened my mouth several times to talk, and so far, nothing's come out. Nothing of importance anyway. I glance at Fallon's plate and see that she's pushing her food around with her fork. She's eaten very little, which concerns me because I know she was hungry. Her whole 'I could eat' facade didn't work like she wanted it to. Maybe she forgot, but I didn't... she used to always say that when she was starving.

"Something wrong with the food?" I ask her.

She shakes her head. I contemplate shutting up but decide to dive in. If things keep going as they are, we'll never talk and I'll have to leave, which will only solidify what she thinks of me.

"Let's just get this over with," I suggest, a little harsher than I intend. "What do you need from me to feel better about accepting my help?"

Fallon sets her fork down and leans back in her chair. "Is that how it's going to be? You blindly repeating what you know I want to hear? Because if it is, I don't see the point."

"Of course you don't. You're holding onto a stupid grudge over a relationship that never was. I left. Get over it."

"I loved you!"

"You were sixteen," I counter hotly. "It was puppy love." Taking a deep breath, I decide to throw out there the one thing that may get her off my back. "In case you've forgotten, I offered to take you with me that day. You *chose* to stay."

"Oh I remember. How could I forget a guilt-ridden offer like that. You were counting on me saying 'no', so let's not pretend otherwise." She breathes deeply. "Besides, if we meant nothing to you, if *I* meant nothing, then why'd you come back? Why the fuck are you here?"

That question stops me dead. There are so many reasons why I'm here, none of which I was prepared to tell her. I should've known the question would come, and on some level, I did. I'd just naively hoped it wouldn't.

Rather than give her every single reason, I give her one I hope satisfies her. "I'm here to make up for leaving. I owe it to you to keep you safe. I couldn't do that before, but I can now."

"Guilt? That's why you drove God only knows how many miles to get here? That's supposed to explain how you knew to come in the first place?" She shakes her head frantically. "I don't fucking think so, David. I may have accepted flimsy explanations up until this point, but no more. I deserve the truth. All of it."

I stand from the table and pick up my plate. I nod at hers and she shakes her head. Good, at least she plans on eating more. While I carry my dirty dishes to the sink, I think about how best to answer her.

When I return to the table, I don't sit. Instead I pace back and forth behind my chair.

"First of all, when I left eight years ago, it had nothing to do with you." I brace my mom on the back of the chair and stare at Fallon. "I left to ensure my ass didn't land in jail for beating the shit out of Ben, or worse. Do you honestly believe I wanted to leave you or my mom? Fuck no, I didn't! That's why I..."

Breaking eye contact, I start pacing again, running a hand through my hair, not giving a shit how messed up it gets. This is exactly what I was afraid of. Fallon would get me so worked up, I spit out shit I had no intention of telling her.

"Why you what, David?" Her tone is quiet, controlled, maybe even a little hopeful. "That's why you what?"

I heave a sigh and face her again. "It's why I've followed your every move, tracked you in the papers, on social media. That's why I never stopped watching out for you."

"And your mom?"

"Of course."

"So, you're telling me you've monitored me from afar?"

I nod. "Every single day I had a routine. I scrubbed the internet for any news in any town you lived in, as well as wherever my mom is. I've followed the news from back home, where we both escaped from. I've watched your social media daily, kept track of your education, all of it. I never stopped giving a damn about you."

"Why didn't you call or write or email? If you cared so much, why didn't you contact me in any way, shape, or form?"

"Would it have mattered?"

"Yeah, it would have. More than you can imagine."

My head falls and I try to fill my lungs with a shaky breath. "I'm sorry, Fallon. I really am. Not for leaving, because I definitely wouldn't have been any good to you from the inside of a prison cell, but I'm sorry for the way I handled it, for the way it hurt you."

"It didn't hurt—"

"Don't," I snap. "You wanted honesty, and I'm giving it to you. I think I deserve the same."

Fallon lowers her eyes, and when she opens them to look at me, the depth of pain I see in her green irises guts me. A tear streaks down her cheek, and she swipes it away.

"You want honest? Because I can do honest."

"Yes, Fallon, I do."

She rises from her chair and pushes it under the table once she's standing. While she carries her plate to the trash to dump the rest of her meal, she says, "It hurt more than I thought possible when you left. Maybe you're right and it was puppy love, but it was still real. I relived the moment I watched you ride off into the sunset with every single beating after that and blamed you for them all. I tried to be interested in other boys, other men, but I couldn't. Because you were always here." She presses a hand to her chest. "Always. I couldn't fuck you away, I couldn't educate you away, I couldn't do a damn thing because, for whatever reason, my soul latched onto you the second you walked into my house after our parents got married, and no matter how hard I've tried, it won't let go."

She throws her now empty plate into the sink, and it shatters, breaking the brief silence following her outburst. With her hands braced on the edge of the counter, she bends over and appears to be holding on for dear life. I take a few steps toward her but halt when she straightens, and whirls around to face me, her eyes brimming with tears.

"How's that for fucking honest?"

"I, uh..."

"This is why I don't want you here. Because I can pretend that you don't exist when you're not standing in front of me." Fallon gestures up and down at my body. "But this... you looking like a deer in headlights, not knowing what to say, close enough for me to reach out and touch you? I don't know how to handle this."

My mind spins, round and round in circles as I try to process everything she's said. None of it makes sense, yet...

"What if I told you it hasn't been easy for me either?"

"Bullshit," she scoffs. Her eyes travel from my head to my toes and back again. "You probably have women falling at your feet."

I can't stop the grin that comes in response to her perusal of me. "You're not wrong," I say in an effort to lighten the mood.

It doesn't work.

"Not helping," she seethes.

"Listen, all I'm saying is the last eight years hasn't been so different for me in that respect." Throwing caution to the wind, I close the distance between us and lift her chin with my finger, so she's forced to maintain eye contact with me. "I'm not going to lie and tell you I loved you back then because I don't know exactly what the feeling was. I *do* know it wasn't nothing. And that kiss we shared, it meant something. With you, I definitely had more than I bargained for, and that scared the shit out of me."

Fallon's shoulders slump. "Why?"

"Because I knew you would be the only one who could make me stay." I shift my hand to cup her cheek. "Despite

69

what you thought, or still think, or how it seemed, I cared about you then and I care about you now. That will never change."

Fallon leans into my touch for a moment but then pulls away and squares her shoulders. "None of this soul-baring changes anything. I'm glad I have your side of the story, so to speak, but it doesn't do us any good. You want to protect me. I don't need, or want, your protection. End of story."

Anger flares at her callous summation, and I find myself wanting to throttle her.

Fallon isn't one of your brothers. You can't lash out at her because she's pissed you off.

"Why are you so—"

The buzzing of the intercom at her door is loud and insistent. I've never lived in a building like this, but I'm pretty sure the doorman isn't supposed to sit on the damn thing.

Fallon rushes to answer it. "Yes?"

"There's a delivery here for you, ma'am. They're saying it requires a signature."

Fallon glances over her shoulder at me and arches a brow. "Did they say where the delivery is from?"

"Hold on a second, ma'am, and I'll check."

"Did you order anything?" I ask while she waits. She shakes her head and immediately the hairs on the back of my neck stand up. "Don't let them—"

"The man says it's paperwork from your accountant, ma'am."

My nerves calm slightly as I remember her accountant talking about sending something to her to sign at the end of their meeting earlier today.

"Thank you. I'll be right down."

Fallon opens her door, and I quickly follow her out of

the apartment. While we're in the elevator, there's tension, but it's different somehow.

"Thank you," I say quietly.

She lifts her head and looks at me. "For?"

"For not having them come up to the apartment."

"Don't mention it."

When the elevator doors slide open, Fallon steps out. I do the same but run into her when she stops in her tracks. I follow her gaze to see why.

My blood boils and my heart threatens to beat out of my chest when my eyes land on the figure in the corner. His head is lowered, obstructed by a ball cap, but his stance, the way he carries himself, standing there like he owns the place. I'd recognize Ben anywhere.

I bend so I can whisper in her ear.

"Does this change anything?"

CHAPTER 11
FALLON

C hills dance up my spine like figure skaters going for the gold. That coupled with the scorching heat coming from Toga is enough to shock my system.

"Miss Fallon, are you okay?" The doorman moves toward me, and I press myself back against Toga.

"Y-yes. I'm fine."

I should be screaming 'call the police', but after that phone call with Snow, I'm not really sure there's any point in that. My father clearly has access to the money required to get away with whatever he wants. I don't know that I can fight that, fight him.

Fuck! I'm gonna have to go to Denver, Colorado, aren't I?

"Get back on the elevator," Toga commands. I shake my head. I'm not running, not from this situation. "Fallon." He drawls out my name with a large dose of warning.

I take a deep breath and then several more before forcing my feet to move and walk forward a few steps, toward my father.

72

"What are you doing here?" My words come out shakier than I intended.

"Ma'am, I'm just here to deliver these." Dad thrusts the large envelope at me without making eye contact. "From your accountant."

I yank the 'documents' out of his hand. I don't for a second believe they're from my accountant, but I also don't believe he'd risk coming here to give me blank papers. Ben knows I won't make a scene, not where I live, so what gives? What the hell is he up to?

Turning to walk back to the elevators, his voice stops me in my tracks.

"Miss Hart?"

Tilting my head back to stare at the ceiling, I hear rather than see Toga stepping next to me.

"You're done here," Toga commands as he grabs my arm to pull me further away from Ben.

"Miss Hart, your accountant said to tell you this won't be the last set of documents he sends." Toga bristles and I shiver. "He said to warn you that he's not done with you."

The tension in the lobby of my building is so high I fear the place will explode because it has nowhere to go. Just like me, there's no escape. The warning is clear: my father isn't done with me, not by a long shot.

Toga's giving you an escape.

Toga pulls away from me, and my attempt to stop him fails. I twist around to watch as he marches toward my father and lifts him up by the lapels of his jacket to slam him into the wall. My doorman gasps and goes for the phone, but Toga's on it.

"I wouldn't do that if I were you," he warns. "We're just having a friendly conversation here. Besides, what would the other tenants think when cops start showing up?"

The doorman slinks back, annoyance and fear flashing on his face. I don't blame him. I'm annoyed and scared, and I know these people.

I return my attention back to Toga and Ben. Ben isn't saying a word or putting up a fight, but the grin on his face says he's not going to let this go. The question is, who will he take it out on? Toga or me?

"You're lucky we're in the building where your daughter lives, asshole," Toga seethes. "If we were anywhere else, you'd have been dead the moment I laid eyes on you."

"Now, Son, is that any way to talk to your father?"

Toga hauls back an arm and lands a blow to Ben's face. Again, Ben does nothing. He lets the blood drip from his nose, and his grin widens to flash red stained teeth.

"I'm not your son." Toga's tone oozes disgust. "I never was. And you're certainly not a man who deserves to be called 'father'."

"You're right." Dad looks at me. "I prefer 'Daddy'."

Toga grips his chin and forces my father to look at him. His skin turns white around Toga's fingers.

"Motherfucker, you don't get to look at her, not after what you did." Toga hauls him off the wall and thrusts him toward the door. "Get the fuck out of here before I change my mind."

Ben makes a show about adjusting his jacket and feeling his face for injuries. He pushes open the door but pauses to look over his shoulder... at me. "I'll be back. With another package from your accountant, of course."

With that, he disappears outside. Toga's body relaxes slightly, and he returns to my side.

"Are you okay?" he asks as he brushes a finger over my cheek.

I nod.

"Miss Fallon, can I get you anything?" the doorman asks, slowly peeling himself from the wall as if just remembering he's on the clock.

"I'm fine, thank you," I assure him.

"Actually," Toga insists. "You can never buzz Miss Fallon's apartment again if that man shows up. Or call the cops and have that son of a bitch trespassed from the property."

"That's a good idea, sir. I think calling the cops is the right thing to do." The doorman picks up the phone, but before he can dial, Toga reaches across the counter and depresses the button.

"If you do, be prepared to handle them on your own. Miss Fallon won't be speaking to them."

"But... I... That makes no sense."

"It doesn't have to make sense. It's just how it's going to be."

With that, Toga wraps an arm around me and ushers me to the elevator. Neither of us say a word until we're back inside my apartment with the door locked behind us.

"So..." he says to finally break the silence.

"So..."

Toga cups my cheeks and gently caresses them with his thumbs. "Fallon, I think this changes things."

My brain shouts at me to tell him he's wrong, that I can handle whatever my father throws my way. But my gut, and my heart, win out, and I burst into tears. Leaning into his chest, I savor the moment his arms come around me to provide the comfort I make it so hard to give.

"It changes everything," I cry into his chest.

Toga holds me as the tears continue to come, as they soak his skin in salty resignation. He rubs my back, croons 'it'll be okay' over and over again. He does everything right.

Why then, is it so hard for me to accept that it isn't just out of guilt?

Because he could simply walk away, return to his life and free himself of the burden. But he chooses to stay. He came on his own and he's still here.

Once the tears subside and I catch my breath, I realize I'm still holding the manilla envelope my father gave me. I push away from Toga to sit on the couch, dropping it on the coffee table as I do.

"We need to see what's in there?" Toga nods at the envelope as he sits next to me.

"I know."

"You don't have to look at it if you don't want to."

My stubbornness kicks in and I snatch it off the table. I tear the top off and toss the scrap of paper on the floor. When I pull out the stapled packet and skim through it, my heart drops.

"Oh my God."

"What is it?" Toga rips the packet from my hands to see for himself.

"It's everything," I whisper in disbelief. "Fucking everything."

Toga's gaze bounces between the pages and me. Judging by the look on his face, he's in as much shock as I am.

"How did he get all this?" Toga points to the top page before flipping to the next. "There's bank records, property records, stuff about your nonprofit and background on your Board of Directors, info about the money your mom left you, GPS history... Your entire life is right here."

"How did you know about the money?" I ask, confused.

Toga's eyes narrow and he just stares at me while I put the pieces together.

"Right. You did your homework."

"Exactly," he confirms. "And it seems Ben did his. But how?"

"Like Snow said, loan sharks." I stick my hand out for the papers and Toga gives them to me. I flip through them again. "But this is bigger than loan sharks, right? I mean, who in their right mind, criminal or not, would loan him the amount of money it would take to get this kinda info?"

"I'll have Brady get on it and see what more he can find. It might be nothing, but hopefully he'll at least come up with a lead."

I nod because that's all I'm capable of. My entire world started to fall a few weeks ago, but somehow, it didn't crumble to the ground. I withstood the hurricane. Now, within a matter of minutes, I have no clue how to remain standing. My world as I know it is officially destroyed.

Unless...

I drop the papers on the table and twist to face him.

"You win, Toga. I'll go to Colorado."

CHAPTER 12
TOGA

Meetings. Packing. Phone calls. Planning.

So much goddamn planning over the last two days. And all of it led up to this moment: Fallon and me in a new truck, with a U-Haul attached to the back, on our way to Denver.

When Fallon agreed to come with me, I had no clue what that meant for her, all the things she'd need to take care of to make it happen. Now I do. And shit, I'm exhausted, and all I did was the heavy lifting.

Aside from her independence and deep seeded anger with me, Fallon had good reasons to stay in California. Source of Love being the biggest. It opens in just over a month, and it is going to be infinitely harder for her to handle from afar. But I believe in her. Especially after seeing how efficient she was trying to arrange for every possible scenario.

Fallon is amazing, smart, beautiful, stubborn, and perfectly capable of doing whatever she sets her mind to. She's proved that.

"I'm hungry."

I glance at her, sitting in the passenger seat with a pillow propped between her and the window, dressed in black leggings and a gray hoodie. Her feet are warm in cozy socks, and her boots are in a heap on the floor. Even like this, she's perfect.

"There's an exit in a few miles. We'll stop there," I tell her.

"Thanks."

Fallon lifts her cell phone from her lap and starts scrolling. It's quiet until we pull into the parking lot of a little diner.

"You've got to be kidding me!" She buries her face in her pillow and screams. When she comes up for air, she turns her cell so I can read the screen. "Can you believe it? Fucking delays. Most of my stuff is now going to take two weeks to get there."

I grab her hand and lower it so I can look her in the eyes. "It'll be okay, I promise. We've got the necessities in the U-Haul. Most of what you'll be waiting on is furniture, and I've got plenty at my place."

"You make an awful lot of promises, ya know that?" she huffs as she tugs on her boots and gets out of the truck, slamming the door behind her.

"Only to you, Kid. Only to you," I mumble under my breath.

We take our time eating, and it's an hour and a half before we're on the road again. Within minutes, Fallon is asleep. I wait another thirty minutes to make a phone call.

"Hello?"

"Hey, Laney. Got a minute?"

A brief rustling comes through the line and what sounds like the voice of a man in the background. But before I can give her a hard time about that, the background noise disappears.

"For you, Toga, I've got ten." She chuckles. "What's up?"

I assure myself that Fallon is still asleep and then answer. "We're headed home, and I need a favor."

"'We'? You mean I'm going to get to meet the girlfriend?"

"Fallon isn't my girlfriend," I insist.

And it's the truth. She isn't. Hell, I don't know what she is, but we definitely haven't put any labels on it. She's a friend, sure, a part of my past life. And she's someone I care about more than I should or that makes sense. But not my girlfriend.

"You can deny it all you want, but Magic explained things to all of us." And there's one fight when I get back. "Besides, you need a woman in your life. You're too, I don't know, hard sometimes."

I heave a sigh and try to keep the annoyance at bay. "Can you do me a favor or not?"

"Sure, what is it?"

"Can you head over to my place and make sure it's fit for a chick? Check the fridge and see that there's food? Shit like that?"

"Of course I can. When do you think you'll be here?"

"Tomorrow sometime. We're gonna stop for the night at some point. It's been crazy the last few days, and we both need some rest where we're not looking over our shoulders or waiting for someone to show up, if you know what I mean?"

"I do. I'll take care of it, Toga. You take care of her and don't worry. Everything here will be ready."

"Thanks, Laney. I appreciate it."

"No problem."

"Oh, and one more thing," I say before disconnecting the call.

"What's that?"

"Tell Magic to watch his back. I'm coming for him when we get there."

I lower the phone to hit the end button and hear her gasp. It crosses my mind to ask her what that's all about, but I dismiss it. It doesn't matter. Laney is Snow's sister, but she's like a sister to all of us and no doubt she's worried about Magic's safety because she knows I can whoop his ass with my hands tied behind my back.

That call out of the way, I'm able to relax a little. It feels like a lifetime has passed since I left my house and I was worried about the state I left it in, now that Fallon is with me. But Laney won't let me down.

Two hours later, Fallon wakes up and stretches. She flattens her palms on the ceiling of the truck and groans as she tries to work out the kinks in her upper body.

"Have a good nap?"

"Uh huh." She twists in her seat and draws her knees up to her chest. "So, Laney is Snow's sister, right?"

"She is," I respond, suspicion knotting my gut. "Why?"

"What kind of food does she like?"

I glance at her before refocusing on the road. "Regular food, I guess. Meat, potatoes, salads." I shrug. "Normal stuff. Why?"

"If she's going to be stocking the fridge and getting your place ready, I was just curious as to what I can expect to eat when we get there."

"I thought you were asleep," I accuse. Not because I care that she overheard but because I feel stupid at having been caught.

"I was. But you're not exactly a quiet person, Toga."

"Fine," I concede with a laugh. "When I left, it was the start to my weekend off. I planned on going to the store and cleaning and shit, but then I read the paper and took off like a bat outta hell. My place is probably a wreck. There, ya happy?"

"Little bit, yeah."

"Glad I could be of service."

Fallon laughs at that and repositions herself so she's facing forward. I try to focus on the road, but I'm keenly aware of every tiny movement of hers, every breath, every hair on her head, and it's difficult to ignore.

I can feel her glancing at me every few seconds, and it's unnerving.

"What is it?"

"I, uh..." She grabs her pillow. "Care if I rest my head on your lap, stretch out a bit?"

Hell no, I don't care! Get as close to my lap as you can. Just be prepared to feel your head being poked.

"Nah, go ahead," I say instead.

She lays her pillow on my legs, which fortunately are long enough that she can fit between me and the steering wheel. Then she lays down and everything around me but her and the road disappears.

Fallon yawns loudly and tucks her arm under the pillow so her fingers graze my thigh through my jeans. I adjust my body as gently as I can and shift one hand from the steering wheel to her side, surprised when she doesn't protest.

Why the hell did you say this was okay?

We stay like that, her resting and me fighting my cock's reaction, for the rest of the day's journey. When I stop at the motel for the night and she sits up so we can check in, I silently mourn the loss of her body against mine.

Maybe, just maybe, I'll get lucky and there will only be a room with one bed available.

Unfortunately, when we unlock the door to the room we're given, I realize I'm not that lucky. My head immediately goes to getting through the night and getting some rest, but my dick isn't on board with that.

"Which bed do you want?" Fallon asks as she steps through the threshold and walks into the room.

Whatever bed you're taking.

"Doesn't matter to me."

As soon as the words are out, I want to call them back. I need the one closest to the door. I *am* supposed to be protecting her, after all.

"I'll take this one." She drops her overnight bag on the mattress closest to the bathroom, and I breathe a sigh of relief. When she faces me, her eyes travel the length of my body, hesitating on my crotch. "You probably want to get a shower, huh?"

"At some point, yeah."

"Okay. I'll grab one after you."

The filter in my brain, the one that controls my mouth, goes on the fritz. "Or we could conserve water."

"Conserve water?" she repeats. Based on the smirk on her face, I know she knows exactly what I mean. "Is that really what you want?"

"No... yes... I don't know." I thrust a hand through my hair and throw my own bag down. "You've got me all tied up in knots, and I have no clue what to do with that. I'm not going to lie and say I don't want you. I do... I mean, what man wouldn't? But do I expect it? No. Will I be upset if you tell me to 'fuck off'? Also no. I get that whatever is between us is weird and undefined and *different*."

"And if I say yes?"

She tilts her head and chews on her bottom lip. It's sexy as fuck, and my cock swells to an impossible size. Or at least it feels like it with the way my jeans are too tight and uncomfortable.

"I'd tell you to be sure."

"And if I'm sure?"

"I'd wonder what's changed."

"I told you, Toga. Everything's changed."

"Has it though?" *Why am I questioning this?* "Just because you agreed to come to Colorado and let me protect you while Ben is out there somewhere doesn't mean anything beyond that has changed." *Quit arguing and take her to the shower, take her in the shower… just take her!* "If you mean it and you really want to take this to the next level, I'm all in. But you have to know that I don't take it lightly. I watched over you all these years for a reason. I came for you for a reason. And it wasn't for a quick lay."

"I know that, and I'm not taking this lightly either. Trying to flirt, yes. Taking it lightly, hell no!" Fallon closes the distance between us and flattens her hands on my chest. "Like I said before, my soul latched onto you years ago, and despite everything, it hasn't let go. There's a reason for that." She rises onto her tiptoes and presses her lips to my ear. "I say we explore all those reasons we keep tossing out there and see where they take us."

That's all I need to hear. I bend to scoop her up and throw her over my shoulder, caveman style, to carry her to the bathroom. With one hand behind her legs, I hold onto her ass with the other. Fuck, that ass. I'm going to make it mine one of these days. But not tonight.

Tonight, I'm just gonna show her that, on a physical level at the very least, we're good together.

CHAPTER 13

FALLON

N aked and wet. How in the hell did I, Fallon Hart, get naked and wet with David Locke?

You said yes to conserving water.

When I agreed, I had visions of him tossing me over his shoulder and carrying me to the shower, where he'd immediately strip me down and have his way with me. I guess I got the tossing me over his shoulder part right. Never in a million years did I think I'd be standing under the hot spray with him washing my hair.

Granted, his cock is jutting out, and he's more than ready. Hell, so am I. But he's taking his time, and I can't help but appreciate that. Even if my pussy is clenching with a burning need I haven't felt for anyone else.

"I think it's clean."

I wrap my fingers around his forearms to lower them to his sides. Rather than follow my lead, he backs me up against the wall and raises my arms above my head.

"It might be, but I'm not done," he growls, and my insides turn to molten lava.

Toga takes the little bar of soap and lathers it between

ANDI RHODES

his hands. He starts at my neck and makes his way to my calves, ignoring the scars while ensuring that his hands touch every part of me but where I want him to. My legs begin to quiver as he slowly shifts closer to my center on his way back up.

Watching his every move, I lock eyes with him when he lifts his head and stares at me from beneath hooded eyes.

"This isn't exactly conserving water," I taunt.

"Nope." Toga finally moves his hand between my legs but stops short of my mound. "I'm gonna do things to you now." He grazes my clit but doesn't stay there.

My hips undulate toward his hand, begging for him to touch me again. Thank heavens, he doesn't keep me waiting. He leans forward and licks my clit with the tip of his tongue, flickers across the sensitive nub with an expertise I wasn't expecting.

I brace my hands on his shoulders to steady myself because I know it won't be long before I explode if he keeps going like he is.

He pauses and commands, "Hands back on the wall."

Shaking my head frantically, I can't get my brain to do as he says.

"Fallon," he warns as he laps at me. The rumble of his voice against my pussy is equally as intoxicating as his tongue.

A split second passes before his chest is pressed against mine, pinning me to the wall. He ensnares my hands in his and forces them upward.

"Do you want to come?" he asks between nibbles on my ear lobe.

I nod.

"Then let me make that happen."

Without letting me go, he crashes his lips against mine

and devours me, feasts on me like a starving animal. The kiss is hot, steamy, full of passion I didn't know existed.

"I need you," I plead into his mouth.

Toga doesn't hesitate. He hoists me up and settles me so all he has to do is thrust into my velvety heat. The second I wrap my legs around him, he does just that.

His cock fills me up, and I throw my head back on a moan. This. This is exactly what I was waiting for. And it's infinitely better than any fantasy I could have conjured up.

"Tight," he groans. "You're so tight."

Toga fucks me like his life depends on it. He dips his head to suck on my tits, and fireworks begin to spark behind my eyelids. He struck the match, lit the wick, and it's a matter of seconds before I see the full display.

I clench around him, and he increases his speed. His hips fly, causing my tailbone to bang into the wall with such force I'm afraid I'll crash through. Before my mind takes hold of that thought, my belly quivers, my pussy clamps down, and the display begins.

"Oh fuuuck," I wail. "Don't stop."

"That's it, baby. Milk me for all I've got."

I don't know how many thrusts it takes, but his movements tense and his dick pulses inside me. We both moan out our release as we're hurdled through the sky amongst the colorful blaze.

When we still, my head collapses on his chest and my body goes limp. Toga maintains his hold on me as he turns off the water and flings the shower curtain aside. He lifts me out and sets me on the counter. He doesn't let go of me, but rather, he steps between my legs and tightens his hold.

"You're right," he finally says. "We didn't conserve water."

I can't stop the very unladylike snort that escapes and his responding chuckle rumbles in his chest.

"No, we didn't. But..."

Toga leans back and lifts my chin with a finger. "But what?"

"That wasn't at all what I expected."

His brow furrows. "No?"

I shake my head. "It was better."

A grin tugs at the corners of his lips, and he allows it to spread.

"And it's only the beginning, Fallon."

SUN STREAMS THROUGH THE CURTAINS. I roll to my side, expecting to find Toga next to me, but when my hand hits an empty bed, I shoot up and lift my arm to block the rays. Toga is standing next to the window, fully dressed. He must sense me because he turns and smiles.

"Mornin'."

"What time is it?"

Toga nods at the clock. "A little after ten."

I throw the blankets off of me and get out of bed. "Shit!" I scramble to find clothes, racing around the room like a crazy person. "We were supposed to leave two hours ago."

Toga leaves his post at the window to stop my search for my bra. He takes my hands in his and forces me to slow down and take a deep breath.

"It's not a big deal," he assures me. "If we absolutely had to leave, I'd have woken you up."

"But you said—"

"I know what I said," he interrupts. "And hitting the road at eight would have been great, but if I'm being honest, I had more fun watching you sleep than I would have driving. Really, it's all good. *And*, we don't have to check out until eleven, so..." His eyes bore into mine, and my toes curl.

"So..."

He threads his hands through my hair and splays his fingers around the back of my neck to pull my mouth close to his.

"So, I can think of a better way to spend the next forty-five minutes than searching for clothes or worrying about the time."

I jump up and he catches me easily so I can lock my legs behind his back. "Works for me."

Forty-seven minutes later, we're both racing around the room to make sure we don't leave anything behind. Not that there is anything. We spent the entire time we were here having sex or sleeping.

After checking out, Toga tosses our stuff on the back floorboard. He helps me into the truck before jogging to the driver's side and sliding in next to me.

"How about breakfast?"

I raise a brow. "You mean lunch, right?"

Toga starts the engine and makes his way out of the parking lot. "Yeah, fine. How 'bout lunch?"

"I could eat." I grin widely.

He shakes his head as he comes to a stop at a light and lets his gaze travel to my core. When he looks me in the eyes again, he smirks.

"So could I."

CHAPTER 14
TOGA

The rest of the drive passes quickly. Just as the sun is going down, I turn onto the road that leads to the Satan's Legacy MC gate.

"We're close, right?" Fallon asks as she puts her boots on.

"Still have a few miles to go, but yeah, we're real close."

And the closer we get, the more my tension eases. The trip has been fun, and I've enjoyed my time with Fallon, but that doesn't mean I let my guard down. I was constantly on alert, watching every vehicle that passed, making sure that we were safe, that *she* was safe.

"I'm sure you're glad to be home."

"Yes and no," I admit. Being home is great, but it opens up another can of worms and that's my lifestyle. What if she sees what I do and hates me for it? What if she can't handle it?

Fallon sits sideways in her seat, and I can feel her eyes burning into the side of my head with questions.

"Spit 'em out, Kid."

"It's just... I guess I don't understand the 'no' part of that answer."

The gate comes into view, and I stop the truck to swipe my ID so the chain link will slide open. After driving through and seeing it close behind us, I pull over to the side of the road and put the truck in park.

"What are you doing?" Fallon asks, glancing around us, confused.

"Listen, Fallon, there are some things you need to know, things I still haven't told you." *Things I'm afraid to tell you.*

"Okay." She drags the word out, her tone wary.

I take a deep breath and dive right in. "You know I'm in a motorcycle club. You met Magic, talked to Snow. You've seen my cut and my patches and my Harley."

"Yeah."

"Do you remember when Snow called me the Sergeant at Arms?"

"Yes."

"Do you know what that means?"

Fallon shrugs. "I guess it means you're someone pretty important in the club."

"That's true, I am." I reach across the seat and link my fingers with hers. "I'm kind of like internal affairs for the club. I handle any issues with members, oversea prospects, dole out punishment... those sorts of things."

"Dole out punishment?"

I nod. "By any means necessary."

"So you hurt them?"

"I do, when it's warranted or when I'm ordered to."

"What about people outside of the club?"

"Same thing. I do what is necessary or what I'm ordered to do to protect the club, and anyone associated with it."

She thinks about it a moment before shrugging. "Okay. Is there anything else I need to know?"

"Well, we're what's known as one percenters. We do bad things, but we're not bad people."

"What bad things?"

Jesus, this has turned into the Spanish Inquisition. I realize my mistake in not telling her any of this earlier, like before we left her apartment. Now I need to speed things up and spit it all out at once.

"Okay, look. I'm just gonna level with you. But first, I need to know that what I tell you won't be repeated. Not only can I get in trouble for telling you, but the safety of a lot of people depend on you keeping it to yourself."

"I won't tell a soul, Toga. I promise."

"Here's what you need to know. There are always going to be things going on that I can't discuss with you, no matter what. That's a hard and fast club rule."

"Got it. Sit in the background and don't ask questions."

"Once you're in the club, you're in. There is no way out other than forcibly being removed or death. And quite frankly, I don't want out and I don't see myself ever wanting that. So you either accept all of this now or we'll figure something else out to make sure you're safe."

"Toga, I wouldn't be here if I didn't want to be. Obviously, I trust you." She squeezes my hand. "I think you're making this harder than it has to be."

"Maybe, but I have to get this stuff out. You deserve to know." I take another deep breath and continue. "Satan's Legacy MC dabbles in gun running, but our main game is drugs. I guess you could compare us to a cartel, only on a much smaller scale. We have other legal businesses that provide us with a front. We party a little too hard, some of us kill time with women. We're rowdy, hardened, and set in our ways. But we're also good people with big hearts, and we do a lot of good for our community."

"Like what?"

"We provide security for several shelters in town, we run a Christmas program and several community events throughout the year for the underprivileged. If you ask anyone in the general public, we're good people who serve Denver."

"But if I ask anyone who's crossed paths with you or is part of your world, you're criminals?"

"Yes, but you're not going to ask, right?"

"Definitely not." She shivers as if the prospect of asking a forbidden question is the most terrifying thing in the world. "Can I ask you one last question?"

"Shoot."

"Do you kill people?"

"I have, yes. And I will again. But they always deserve it."

"That's supposed to make it okay?"

"No. That's supposed to justify it." I pull away and turn slightly forward. "I'm not going to change Fallon. At the end of the day, I am who I am. A patched member of a one percenter motorcycle club who doesn't blink twice at the dirty work. And the man who will never stop protecting you whether you're here or not." I look back at her. "So, can you live with this or not? Because I need to know now."

Fallon again appears to mull over the info I've given her. She looks around at our surroundings and then focuses on me.

"Take me home, Toga. To *your* home."

A feeling of excitement rushes through me. She doesn't hate me or the man that I am.

She hasn't actually seen you in action.

93

I push my traitorous thoughts from my mind and start the truck. I follow the road down the hill and the next half mile to the main clubhouse. Slowing, I take the left that leads us to my house. The porchlight greets us as I park in front of the small three bedroom, two bath structure.

"This is your place?" Fallon asks as she steps out of the truck.

"This is it. Home sweet home."

I stop her when she goes to open the back passenger door. "Why don't I give you the tour and then I'll unload everything?"

"Works for me."

I lead her up the steps and usher her inside after unlocking the door. Laney left a few lights on so Fallon can easily see the layout of the home.

"Here's the living room and, as you can see, the kitchen is right there." I point ahead of us. "Laundry is around the corner off the kitchen."

I take in our surroundings, trying to see the overstuffed leather furniture and large flatscreen TV on the wall as she sees it. It's manly, but could easily feel like home for her... I think. Her apartment wasn't overly girly. There were no floral prints. Sure, her stuff is higher end, but it was still comfortable and homey.

"I like it."

"Let me show you where you'll be sleeping." I grab her hand and walk her toward the hall.

"I assume I'll just have to follow you to bed, right? Because I'll be sleeping with you."

"I can make that happen." My insecurities start to filter in. "But I'll show you the second room, just in case." I point to the left. "Here's the first bathroom. Pretty basic." I turn

94

her to the right. "And here's the room I had Laney make up for you."

When I flip on the light, I can see Laney did exactly as I asked. She made it fit for a chick. One who's older with a lot of cats, maybe, but certainly not for Fallon.

"Wow," Fallon says with a chuckle. "Never realized how much I hated flowers until just now."

"Right." I remind myself to ask Laney what she was thinking later. "My room it is."

Fallon turns to wrap her arms around my waist and lifts her eyes to my face. "Perfect." She stands on her tiptoes and presses her lips against mine, giving me a slow kiss.

Taking advantage of the situation, I lift her into my arms, never breaking the connection, and carry her to my— no, now it's *our*—room. I toss her onto the mattress and quickly strip my shirt over my head. I lean over to hook my thumbs into the waistband of her leggings and yank them off her legs.

Just as Fallon sits up and reaches for my belt, my front door being opened reverberates through the house.

"Toga, Fallon, where are you guys?" Magic calls out.

"We really need to work on some boundaries with him," Fallon states, bending over the bed to reach for her discarded leggings.

"I'm on it."

Magic's footsteps echo through the house, and before he can reach this room, I rush out to the hall in time to see him poking his head into the bathroom.

"Really, bro?" I ask, arms crossed over my chest, legs braced apart. "Just gonna take it upon yourself to fucking search my house?"

Magic's head pops out into the hall as he straightens and he's sporting a grin. He shrugs. "Sure, why not?"

"Why not?" I repeat. "Why fucking not?! How about because it's my place? Or how about because you know damn good and well, I'm not alone in here?"

"That's never stopped either one of us." The door behind us opens, and Magic leans to the side to look at Fallon. "Hey. Long time no see."

"Hi Magic."

"I have to say, with the way you two were when I left Cali, I was not expecting you to be coming out of the same bedroom."

"And I'd have to say..." Fallon begins as she walks around us. "... butt the fuck out."

"Roger that."

"Jesus Christ," I mumble. "Why are you here, Magic?"

"Oh, man, you mean you didn't miss me?" he teases.

"Sure, I missed you. Now, what do you want?" I enunciate each word, giving him every indication that I'm not in the mood. I was about to have more of the best sex of my life, and his stupid ass ruined it.

"I'm on security tonight, monitoring the cameras and the gate. I saw you drive in with the U-Haul and figured you could use the help." He starts backing up toward the front door. "Guess I was wrong."

"No, wait." I walk out into the open space and wave my arm for him to join us in the kitchen. "You're right, I could use your help." Seeing the beer in Fallon's hand, I silently thank Laney. I grab two more from the fridge and hand one to Magic. "Next time, call first."

Magic takes a long pull from the bottle before setting it on the counter. "Yeah, sorry about that."

"It's fine, Magic," Fallon says. "We hadn't even started yet."

I whip my head around to face her. "Seriously?"

"What?" Her tone drips with innocence, but the smirk on her face gives away the minx in her.

"Do I really have to worry about you two gabbing like teenagers about our sex life?" I glance back and forth between the two waiting for an answer.

"Calm down, Toga," Magic suggests. "You know I don't gab like a teenager. I gossip, like a man."

Fallon throws her head back in a laugh.

"You're both gonna be the death of me." I pin my stare on Fallon. "And you. Is that really what you call 'haven't even started'?" I don't give her a chance to answer. "Because baby, my kickstand was lifted, my engine started, and my throttle was just waiting for you to do your thing." I take a swig of beer and shake my head. "Hadn't even started, my fucking ass."

"Too much info, bro."

"You started it."

Holy shit, now I'm acting just as childish as they are. If this is how things are going to be, I'm not sure I'm up for it.

"Boys, go unload the U-Haul so Magic can go home and we..." Fallon wags her fingers between us. "... can pick up where we left off."

"Toga, you are one lucky son of a bitch, ya know that?"

I smile and don't take my eyes off of Fallon.

"Yeah, I know."

CHAPTER 15

FALLON

"They're gonna be here any minute."

Toga's arms come around me from behind, and I lock eyes with him in the mirror. I've been here for almost a week, and we seem to have settled into some sort of routine. He takes care of club business, and I handle conference calls and all things non-profit. We eat dinner together, when we can, and watch a little television or a movie before going to bed together and waking up together. And all the fun we have in between? That's the icing on the cake of life.

"I know." I frown at my reflection.

"You look incredible, Fallon." Toga leans forward and kisses me on the cheek. "Besides, you're going to be hanging out with the girls, not out trolling for men." He spins me around and looks me dead in the eye. "At least you better not be."

I swat his arm. "You know I'm not."

"Good, because I don't share. Not ever. If you want to see my dark side, that would be a sure-fire way to do it."

"While your dark side intrigues me, even turns me on a

little, I'm in no way going to coax it out that way." She gives me a peck on the lips. "I don't share either. And in case you missed the memo, you're mine, David Locke. All mine."

"Glad we got that cleared up." He grins at me one last time before leaving the bathroom and me alone to finish getting ready.

It doesn't take me but five more minutes, and when I go out into the living room, Laney and Sami are already there, chatting with Toga. Magic and Snow are there, as well as Duck, Dip, and Brady. I've met them all, and many others, but this seems to be the core group of club members.

"Wow, the whole crew is here," I observe. "What's the occasion? I thought this was a girl's night."

"That's the thing around here, honey," Laney says. "Ya always gotta be prepared for plans to change."

"So, not a girl's night?"

"Not technically," Sami confirms. "We have instructed the men to steer clear, but we'll all be at the clubhouse tonight. They've got some business to attend to, so hopefully we'll be good and drunk by the time they join us. It's not often we have a babysitter, and I, for one, plan to take full advantage of that."

"I'm game for whatever," I tell them. "As long as there's beer in my hand and you girls to hang with, I'm down."

I glance at Toga and see him smiling, all the while his eyes are on me. I don't know if this is exactly what Laney said and the plans just changed or if this was some sort of test to see if I fit in. Either way, I think I passed.

Everyone starts to file out of the house. Toga locks the door and leads me down the steps toward his Harley parked in front. Snow and Sami get on Snow's Harley, while Magic and Laney get on his. I, however, stop in my tracks.

"Uh, I'm not getting on that."

"Yeah, you are."

"No, Toga. I can't ride on a motorcycle."

"Toga, bro, you haven't taken her on your bike yet?" Duck taunts. "What the hell? You guys have been here for almost a week. That's sacrilege, man."

"When the fuck has there been time?" Toga counters. "I've been running my ass off for the club, and she's had meetings. It's not like I haven't wanted to."

"Regardless," I interrupt. "I'm not getting on that. Not when we'll be drinking. How will we get home?"

"Fallon, honey, you'll walk home if you have to," Laney informs me. She wraps her arms around Magic's midsection. "Trust me, you want to get on that bike."

Something about the way she says it, about the way she hugs the biker in front of her, strikes me as odd. I dismiss it though. If they're together, it's none of my business, unless they make it my business. Besides, maybe it's against code or something and they don't want anyone to know.

Toga tugs me by the hand. "C'mon, Kid. You can trust me. I haven't let you down so far, have I?"

I eye the motorcycle skeptically. "No, you haven't."

"Then what have you got to lose?" Snow asks from his own bike.

"My life, that's what," I snap.

A hushed silence flows over all of us, making it sink in that I just smarted off to the president. Not my finest hour, but when Snow throws his head back and laughs, I realize it's not my worst either.

Toga swings his leg over the seat. "Are you coming or what?"

I huff out a breath. "Not like this, I'm not." Toga gets my meaning and grins. I throw my leg over to sit behind him, my hands braced on his shoulders. I lean into his ear and whisper, "But we definitely should try it sometime."

"That's my girl."

Engines rev as the rest of the guys get on their bikes, and we take off toward the clubhouse. It's not lost on me that we could have walked there just as easily as we can walk back, but even I have to admit I'm glad we didn't. A girl could get used to having a sexy man to straddle, the wind in her hair, and the vibrations between her legs.

Toga's hand doesn't leave my thigh for the two minutes it takes to ride to the clubhouse and park. After he gets off the bike, he helps me, and then it's his turn to whisper.

"Definitely going to try it later." He kisses my forehead. "So long as someone doesn't get too wasted."

"I don't get wasted."

"Fallon Hart, are you forgetting I've seen your social media accounts?"

"Okay, fine. I've gotten wasted and loved it. But that was back in college."

"Which wasn't all that long ago," he reminds me.

"Feels like a lifetime ago."

Toga guides me inside the clubhouse. "I know it does."

Time for talk is over as Toga is whisked away by the guys and Laney and Sami usher me to the bar. There are other club members here, music in the background, but it isn't too rowdy. Maybe I'm missing something, but this isn't the rager I was picturing. And maybe it's just too early.

When we reach the bar, rather than sit, Laney goes behind the marred wooden bar top. "What can I get ya?"

"I'll take a shot of tequila with a margarita chaser," Sami says in a bubbly voice.

"Girl, I don't know how you managed to talk Snow into

getting that girly shit in here. I've been begging him for years to stock more than just local brews and cheap liquor."

"And he wouldn't get it for you?" I ask.

"Look around, Fallon. We're not exactly brimming with estrogen."

"True. I guess I just thought, as his sister and club princess, you'd have a say in how things are run. Especially if it doesn't affect club business."

"Toga is teaching you well." Laney makes Sami's drink. "I do have a say, in some things. But my brother wins most of the time. I pick and choose my battles, and seeing as I don't drink like he does, this wasn't one I wanted to dig in deep with."

"Makes sense."

Laney and Sami laugh. "No," Laney says. "It doesn't. But the longer you're here, the more it will. So, what'll you have to drink?"

"I'll take a shot of tequila and a whiskey sour."

"Coming right up."

After getting my drinks, Laney gets her own: shot of Jack Daniels and a beer. We each down our shots, after toasting to friendship and things we don't understand, and then we settle in at one of the tables. As we're sitting down, the door opens and someone I haven't met before walks in. He's wearing the same cut, but he's missing a few patches.

"Who's that?" I ask, pointing at him.

"Oh, that's Little Man," Sami informs me. "He's a newer prospect."

"Little Man," Laney calls out to him. "C'mere a minute."

Little Man isn't so little, and I can see his muscles bunch beneath his T-shirt as he saunters over to us.

"What can I do for you, Laney?" His voice is deep, rich, and he talks with a strong southern accent.

Laney smiles and it brightens up her entire face. Hell, it brightens up the whole room and that's saying something considering it's painted completely black with only green accents in the logo on the wall.

"I wanted to introduce you to someone. Little Man, this is Fallon. Fallon, this is Little Man."

He turns to me and lets his eyes fall to my cleavage. Before I can even process what's happening, Laney is out of her chair and around the table. The crack of her palm hitting his cheek echoes in the dark room. Little Man scowls at her, but otherwise, remains silent.

"Fallon is Toga's girl. I don't know about you, but I certainly don't want to have to tell him you were eye fucking her."

"No, ma'am."

"Oh, cut the ma'am bullshit. You know I hate that. Just don't let it happen again. She's taken." Laney shakes out her hand and chuckles. "Jesus, Little Man, what'd you do, implant your cheeks with boulders? That fucking hurt."

"No boulders. That's all me in there." He grins at her, apparently accepting that I'm off limits but still wanting to test the waters elsewhere.

"Go work the bar," Laney instructs. "The others will be here later."

Little Man walks away, but Laney stops him with one last demand. "And grab us another round, will ya?"

"Sure thing, Laney."

After Little Man brings our drinks and sets them in front of us, Laney sits down. She reaches across the table and lifts my hand.

"Sorry, honey."

"For what?"

She nods toward the prospect. "That's probably gonna get ugly later. I'm gonna have to tell Snow what happened."

I let her words sink in, and the longer I think about it, the less I care. Toga warned me about what would happen if another member, or any man for that matter, crossed a line. For the club, his ogling crossed a line. Little Man had to have known what would happen. While I don't think he would have done it if he'd known who I was ahead of time, it doesn't change the facts.

And the facts are: he crossed a line, he has to suffer the consequences, and *I'm* going to get to see Toga's bad side. Which I'm fully expecting to be hot as hell and just the thing to end the night.

CHAPTER 16
TOGA

"Man, it's not good."

I pace the room where church is held and do my best to keep my temper on lockdown. My brothers don't deserve my wrath. No, that's reserved for Ben. And the more I learn, the more he does to hurt Fallon, the more I can guarantee his fate will be ugly, calculated, and violent.

"Spit it out, Brady," Snow commands, slamming his fist into the table. "We don't have all day here."

"Right, well..." Brady shifts in his chair. He's a patched member of Satan's Legacy MC, but perhaps the most reserved. He's kind of a nerd. But Brady is a good dude, and I trust him with my life, with Fallon's life. "He's here, in Denver. I put some feelers out when you and Fallon arrived, and Ben was spotted yesterday at a grocery store."

"How the fuck did this happen?!" Magic shouts, shooting up from his chair. "They bought a new truck with cash, didn't use any credit cards, no forwarding address, nothing. All precautions were taken so this wouldn't happen."

"I haven't quite figured that out," Brady admits.

"You better get it figured the fuck out and soon," Snow commands. "Because I'm not sure how much I can hold Toga back if you don't."

I stick my fingers between my lips and give a shrill whistle. Everyone shuts up and focuses on me. While my blood is threatening to boil through my skin, I also see the possibilities this brings.

"It's okay," I tell them. "This is good."

"How in the hell is this good?" Duck, our Vice President, asks. "He followed you here, which means not only is he not giving up, but he's better than we thought."

"That's just it, he's not better. Ben Hart is either the dumbest man on planet Earth or way too cocky for his own good." When they all stare at me like I've lost my mind, I continue. "Don't you get it? He's on our turf now. Satan's Legacy doesn't lose in Denver. He's going down and probably much sooner than he would have had he stayed away."

"Okay." Duck concedes. "I get that, brother. But what about Fallon? Won't this freak her out? What if she insists on going back to California now that he's here?"

He's right, that's a possibility, but a highly unlikely one. Fallon and I have gotten so much closer since she's been here, and I don't see that changing. I could be wrong, but that's a chance I'm willing to take. I refuse to keep secrets from her, at least when the info is about her.

"She won't."

"How can you be so sure?" Dip, our Road Captain, asks with genuine curiosity.

"He's not sure," Magic answers before I get a chance to. "But he loves her so he's willing to take the risk."

"Whoa, dude." Now it's Duck's turn to whistle. "You love her?"

"Jesus, Duck." Snow rolls his eyes. "How have you not seen that? They're together every chance they get, he stays home more than ever, *and* he let her ride on the back of his Harley tonight. You know the rules."

"Yeah, yeah," Duck mumbles. "No woman on the back of your bike unless she's your ol' lady or you plan to make her your ol' lady."

Motherfucker! The rule, such as it is, didn't even cross my mind when I let Fallon ride with me. I just wanted her behind me, legs wrapped tightly against mine, enjoying the Harley the way I do. Or did I? Maybe there is a part of me that wants to be with Fallon for the long haul and this was my subconscious's way of forcing me to think about it.

"Wait!" Duck slaps his hands on the table and stands. "That is the rule, so what's up with Laney riding on the back of Magic's bike? Last I checked, she's not his ol' lady. Shit, they aren't even dating."

I look at Magic and see him try to avert his eyes. He must think better of it because it's a split-second movement and then he locks eyes with Snow.

"Duck, sometimes I wonder why I made you VP." Snow's teasing, but it has the desired effect. Duck sits down and shuts up. "No, Magic and Laney aren't dating. That is also against the rules. But they're family. And the one exception to the female riders' rule is family. C'mon, bro, get it together."

As entertaining as this is, I really want to get to Fallon and the party, so I reign in the conversation.

"Let's get back to the topic at hand," I bark. "I've got a girl to get to."

"Right. Ben." Snow stands up. "Brady, who spotted him at the store?"

"One of our runners, Danny. Said it looked like Ben was stocking up on canned goods and cheap beer."

I can't stop the derisive chuckle. When everyone's eyes land on me again, I explain. "Sorry, but if you knew Ben, you would know that is some sort of evil punishment in and of itself. Asshole doesn't do cheap. Oh no, it's all fine dining and fancy drinking."

"Where would Ben stay? A hotel, rental home... where?"

"Normally I'd say a five-star resort with a spa, but with his grocery list, it sounds like he's definitely not staying at the Ritz. Maybe a campground somewhere."

"Brady, get on that. Check hotels, motels, camping sites... anywhere a man can lay his head at night. Also, I want to know how the hell he tracked them."

"On it."

"For now, we follow all of our security protocols to a T. Once we narrow down where he might be staying, we'll go after him. Until then, keep your heads down, your shenanigans to a minimum, and your eyes sharp." Snow turns to me. "Toga, fill Fallon in so she knows what's happening. Limit your trips to town if you can. If you have club business to attend to, Fallon is to be with a patched member or Laney. Got it?"

"Absolutely, Prez."

"Great." Snow makes his way to the door. "Church is adjourned. Now let's go have some fun."

As soon as Snow opens the door, breaking the sound-proof barrier, thumping music fills the air. The party is in full swing. We all make our way down the hall, into the main room. The space is full of members, prospects, some trusted friends, and, shall we say, less than dressed club whores.

I twist and turn until I spot who I'm looking for. Fallon

is dancing with Laney and Sami, all of whom are surrounded by guys who aren't exactly crossing a line but getting as close to it as humanly possible without threat of violence.

I weave through the crowd, and when she spots me, she taps on Sami's shoulder and points in my direction. Sami then glances around, no doubt searching for Snow. Fallon takes three giant steps toward me and launches herself in my arms, wrapping herself around me like a spider monkey.

"Hey, Kid." I grin at her. "Having fun?"

Fallon giggles. "So much fun." Her words are a little slurred, but not so bad that I think it's time to call it quits. Fallon's demeanor sobers, and she looks at me with purpose. "I have to tell you something," she says, with hushed importance in her tone.

My muscles tense and a million different things pass through my mind as to what she has to tell me. Is she done here? Does she want to go back to Cali? Did she meet someone else in the short time I was in church? Is she, did she, does she... so many possibilities.

"I mean, I don't have to tell you, but I do, ya know?" She tilts her head and looks adorable in the process.

"No, I don't know."

"Laney said it has to be done, that she would have to tell Snow and shit would get ugly."

"Fallon, what the hell is going on?"

She leans in and whispers in my ear. "I think you have to fight tonight."

I rear back, and my muscles go from tense to stiff with blinding rage. "Who the fuck touched you?"

"What?!"

"Fallon, I'm only going to ask you this one more time

and I need an answer." I set her on her feet, and she looks up at me with confusion. "Otherwise, I'm going to start tearing apart every man in this building, one by one, until there's no one left," I snarl. "Who. Touched. You?"

"No one touched me," she cries, but then she lowers her voice and a mischievous grin spreads across her face. "But they did look at my tits."

"Who looked at your tits?" I'm trying to maintain my frustration because she very clearly thinks this is a serious offense within the club. And it is. But I don't have to kill anyone because of it. Touching gets a man killed, looking gets a man an embarrassing beat down.

Fallon huffs out a breath as if she's bored with the conversation. "Little Man did." She perks back up a little. "And guess what?"

"What?"

"He didn't even flinch at my scars." Now this, she's excited about. "I tried to cover them with makeup as best I could, but even I'm not that good. They're still noticeable. And Little Man didn't seem to mind."

I grip her arms and back her up toward a corner so we have as much privacy as possible. Fallon's eyes go wide, and if I'm not mistaken, there's a flash of fear in her irises. When I have her wedged between me and the wall, I take the top hem of her shirt and drag it down, exposing her tits and scars.

"Listen to me, Fallon, and listen good," I growl. When she nods, I lift her breasts in my hands and continue. "These beauties are mine."

I lower my head and suck a nipple into my mouth while pinching the other between my thumb and forefinger. I do this for several seconds before straightening and locking eyes with her.

"All mine, got it?"

Again, she nods. Her nostrils are flaring, and her breathing has quickened.

"Of course Little Man liked what he saw. You're gorgeous. Every last inch of you. And scars or no scars, you're the most beautiful woman I've ever seen. Hell, that any one in here has ever seen."

"Oh, no," she shakes her head. "Laney and Sami are definitely more—"

"No, they're not," I snap, frustrated that she doesn't see herself like I see her. "Sure, they're beautiful, in their own right. But you? You outshine them. Inside and out. Don't ever doubt that."

"But I—"

"Take the compliment, Fallon. Say 'thank you' and accept it."

"Thank you."

"You're welcome." I lift her shirt back into place, and I swear I hear a little whine come from her. I brush it aside. There will be time for more later. "Now, let's go get crazy."

"One more thing," she says, grabbing my arm and stopping me from walking toward the center of the crowd. I arch a brow at her. "Does this mean Little Man won't get punished?"

"Oh, baby, no. Little Man is gonna get a beat down. You belong to me, and I can't let his disrespect stand. Club rules." I shrug. "But he'll walk away from it."

That seems to satisfy her because she takes my hand and drags me away from the wall. We head to the bar first, and I see Little Man behind it. He spots me, and his movements get clumsy. He's uneasy and I like that. I decide to deliver his beat down later, when he's not expecting it, and instead, order both Fallon and me beers: one for her and two for me.

"Thanks, man," I say to Little Man when he slides them across the bar. "Have a good night."

While making our way to the center of the room where Snow and Sami are, as well as Laney and some of the other brothers, I down my first beer. I let the liquid settle and the music take over.

Fallon dances with her back to me and her ass grinding against my junk. My cock responds, and the look she gives me over her shoulder is full of heat and promise. It's gonna be a damn good night.

A few minutes pass by before I realize just how wrong I am. Fallon's cell vibrates in her back pocket, and as she reaches for it, the security alarms for the entire compound start ringing. The shrill noise causes panic in the clubhouse, and those who are familiar with our protocol immediately head to the back of the building to enter the underground safe room. Although, it's much bigger than a room.

It can hold up to two thousand people and it spans the entire length and width of the compound. We designed it that way in case the community ever needed more shelter from fires or other natural disasters. It's never been used for that purpose, but it has kept club members and their families safe from outsiders numerous times.

I grab Fallon's arm and shove her toward Laney. "Go with them! I shout to be heard over the music and alarms. "I'll be there when I can!"

"Toga."

"Fallon, baby, I need you to go so I can do my job!"

"Cmon, Fallon." Laney tries to pull her away from me, but Fallon digs in her feet.

"Toga!" Fallon yells and that's when I really stop and

look at her. Her face has lost all color, and her eyes are full of fear. She turns her cell around to show me. "Look."

As if the alarms weren't bad enough, now I have to contend with this. On her screen is a text with one simple word, one word that shreds any composure I have.

Gotcha.

CHAPTER 17
FALLON

"Fallon, go with Laney. Now!"

People are screaming and running around me, but I'm stuck in a hazy fog, one that threatens to drown me. I see Toga standing in front of me, concern etched in his features, but his mouth isn't opening so it's not him yelling. I glance down at my arm and see a hand on it, gripping it tightly. I follow the length to see who it's attached to and end up staring at Magic.

"I..." I shake my head frantically. "I can't leave Toga."

"Yes, you can. You don't have a choice." Magic's tone is sympathetic but stern. "We need him to help figure out what's going on. Laney will keep you safe. Just go with her."

I nod, not really sure what I'm nodding for. I could be agreeing to kill myself, for all I know, because Magic's words went in one ear and out the other. All I hear is ringing and all my brain keeps flashing in front of my eyes is that word: Gotcha.

"Fallon, honey, c'mon," Laney urges as she pulls me away from Toga.

I go with her, blindly, not understanding what's

happening, not knowing if I'll ever see Toga again. One way or another, my father is behind this, and that never ends well.

When we reach the hallway, some sense of reality sets in. I dig in my heels and look over my shoulder to see Toga near the front door.

"Toga!" I call out to him. He looks back at me, and his expression is full of rage and sadness. He's worried too. "I love you!"

Before he can respond or I can get a read on his reaction, I'm dragged around the corner and toward a set of stairs that lead down under the clubhouse.

"What the hell is going on?" I ask Laney, who still has a hold of me.

"The alarms sounded because there was a breach of the property. The brothers have to search for whoever caused the breach and take care of them." Laney guides me through a steel door at the bottom of the steps. "And we are going down here to the underground safe room until we get the all clear to go back up."

I hear what she's saying, but my mind keeps returning to that text. There's been a breach and, at the same time, I get a text that says 'Gotcha'. Granted it was from an unknown number, but who else could it be from but my father?

We enter a large open room, and Laney steers me to the left where we huddle near the door. Sami is already there, an annoyed look on her face. Everyone that was upstairs has congregated and are talking and acting as if this is nothing, just another day.

"Why tonight?" Sami whines. "I was having so much fun."

"Me too," Laney agrees. "I think we all were. But shit happens. You know that as well as I do."

"I know. But do you have any idea how hard it is to find a babysitter who Snow trusts and who is willing to come to the compound?"

Laney stares at her and gives a half-hearted chuckle. "Yeah, I do. We have the same babysitter, Sami."

"I know, I know. Sorry."

"Speaking of the babysitter, I trust that Snow explained to her how to access the underground safe room?"

"Of course he did. Three times," she laments. "He and the boys even walked her through how to get here and then made her do it by herself and timed how long it took her."

"Good. Then they should be here soon."

"How do you both do this?" I shake my head. "I don't get it, especially with kids."

They both turn to face me, their expressions a cross between understanding and censure.

"Did you mean what you said up there?" Laney asks, pointing toward the ceiling.

"What did I say?"

"You told Toga that you loved him."

As fuzzy as everything else is, I remember that. How could I forget something as important as being the first to say those three words?

"Well, did you mean it?" Sami prods.

"Yes, I did."

"That's how you do it, how you handle shit like this," Laney says matter-of-factly. "Because you love him, and part of loving someone is accepting them and their lifestyle. This may be the first time you're experiencing the safe room and alarms, but I promise you, it won't be the last. If you love him, you get used to it. If you don't, you leave."

There's clear warning in Laney's tone. And why wouldn't there be? They're all a family. The question is, where do I fit in with the family? And furthermore, how do I live with the fact that right now, the threat against them is because of me?

I take a leap of faith, that's how.

"I need to show you guys something." I lift my cell and tap the screen to bring the text back up. When it's visible, I show them. "We're down here because of me. My father sent this. The same man who almost killed me is the cause of all this chaos."

"Okay. So?" Sami asks.

"So?" I repeat. "So? This is my fault," I cry.

"No, honey, it's not." Laney wraps an arm around my shoulder and pulls me toward her for a half hug. "It's the fault of the man who hurt you."

Emotions crash down on me. Sadness that this is what my life has become. Constant running and overwhelming fear. Anger that I was born to a father who doesn't value family. Frustration that Toga is now involved, which means his life is consumed with it too. Everything swirls around me until tears stream down my cheeks and I cry until I can barely breathe.

Laney and Sami rub circles over my back. They tell me it'll be okay over and over again. Whether or not they're trying to convince me or themselves, I don't know. None of what they're doing helps and breathing becomes almost impossible.

"Fallon, you need to stop worrying about how this affects everyone else," Sami says. "Hell, I ended up here because of my ex. And I'm still here. No one blames me for the trouble my ex caused, for the money lost because of him. I'm here and that's never going to change. It will be the same for you."

"Wh-what if Toga h-hates me?"

"Girl, that man looks at you like you're the sun, the moon, *and* the stars. He doesn't have it in him to hate you. He loves you, and no threat is ever going to change that."

"I hate to break this up," Laney says, standing straight. "But here come the boys. Pull yourself together, Fallon."

Some would think Laney's demand is harsh, but not me. I can only imagine how scared the boys must be, and the last thing they need to see is a blubbering woman who can't get her shit together. I take a deep breath and wipe away the tears.

"Mom!" Lennox shouts over the hushed whispers in the room. "Mom, we're here."

He launches himself at Sami. Shiloh is right behind him, leaping toward Laney.

"Hey, there," Laney says with a big smile. "Were you having fun with the babysitter?" As she asks this, she lifts her head to seek out the woman who is supposed to be with the boys. "Where is she?"

"She's eating dust!" Lennox responds, thrusting his fist above his head.

"Yeah," Shiloh agrees.

"Lennox, what did you two do?" Sami's tone is wary. I've heard the stories about Lennox's struggles with his mom, and I can't help but wonder if they're still going on.

"We didn't do nothing," he argues. "She said she wanted to race us down here and we beat her."

"We did," Shiloh says excitedly. "She's probably back in the tunnel somewhere."

Laney shakes her head. "Well, I'm glad you won, but next time, you don't step one foot—no, one toe—outside of your babysitter's sight. You hear me?"

"Aw, mom." The words are drawn out and dramatic.

"Don't 'aw mom' me. We've talked about this, Shiloh. When those alarms go off, you stay with whatever adult you're with and they'll bring you here. What if something happened to you, or her?"

"Moms take all the fun outta life," Lennox complains. "C'mon, Shiloh, let's go talk to some of the men. They'll understand."

The two boys take off, and as we watch them mingle with the others, I spot movement at the door on the opposite wall. I tap Laney and Sami on the shoulder.

"Ah, ladies." I point to the door. "Is that the babysitter?"

The woman looks exhausted and more than a little scared.

"Jesus," Laney mutters. "Sami, we better do damage control."

They walk away from me, mama bears on a mission. I let them do their thing and slide along the wall to sit on the floor. If I don't have them to talk to, I might as well do something to bide my time. Maybe I can even help.

I go into the texting app on my phone so I can respond to my father. I stare at that 'Gotcha' for a solid five minutes before figuring out what I want to say to him.

Keep telling yourself that, old man.

Okay, so maybe that's a little childish, and certainly not the comeback he deserves, but it's all I could come up with. My hope is he'll keep texting me and reveal something, anything, that could allow us to track him down.

Him: Really? Have I taught you nothing?

Me: Probably not the lessons you thought you were teaching me.

Him: I definitely didn't teach you how to mingle with trash.

Annoyance flares through me. Everything he's put me through over the years and that's what he's choosing to focus on? The fact that I'm living with people he considers less than?

Fucking prick.

I could start a war with words on that subject, but I choose not to. It won't get me anywhere but pissed off with a blood pressure problem. Instead, I shift gears and try to get actual information out of him.

Me: Did you cause the alarms?

Him: What do you think?

Me: How did you find me?

Him: I have my ways.

Me: What's your debt up to? No way you've done all of this alone.

Him: Since when do you give a shit about my debts?

Me: I don't. But I am curious about how much money you think you'll be able to get out of me to save your own ass when the time comes.

Him: Ah, there he is. I can see your boy now. The question is, can he see me?

And just like that, I fall into his trap.

Me: Don't you dare hurt him!

Him: And if I do?

Me: You won't just have me to contend with. This entire club will hunt you down and kill you. Maybe I'll get lucky, and they'll let me actually do the honors. Either way, you'll be dead.

Him: Tell me how you really feel.

I start typing out a response but stop when the door to my right crashes open. Toga comes rushing in, and his head swivels in both directions until he spots me. I scramble to my feet as he closes the distance between us.

He rests his chin in my hair and cups the back of my head to hold me close.

"Are you okay?" he asks, his voice a little shaky.

I pull back so I can look into his eyes. "I'm fine, but... how is this possible? How are you here right now? He said he could see you."

"What are you talking about?"

I show him the text exchange with my father. Toga reads it and lets out a guttural shout as he slams his fist into the concrete wall. Blood trickles from his knuckles, but it doesn't seem to faze him.

Unfortunately, Little Man chooses that moment to come up to Toga.

"What's up, man? Anything I can help with?"

Toga pulls his arm back and lands an uppercut to Little Man's jaw. Little Man rears backward. Toga unleashes all of his pent-up anger and frustration on the prospect, and by the time he's done, Little Man is on the floor, bleeding and bruised.

"Whoa, brother, what was that for?" Magic asks as he steps up behind Toga and pulls him away from Little Man.

"He knows what it's for," Toga barks.

"At least tell me he broke some sort of club rule or bro code."

"Of course he did. I don't make a habit of doling out beatings for the hell of it."

"That's right, you don't." Magic grins at me. "Had to check though." He shifts his attention to Little Man. "Get up and get out of here, unless you want more where that came from."

Little Man does as he's told, and I can't help but remember what Toga said about the prospect walking away. At least he stuck to that.

"Now," Magic begins. "What has your nuts in a noose?"

"He orchestrated this, all of it," Toga responds. "He wanted us to think he was here, make us scramble like idiots. But he's not here. Fuck, he's probably not even close."

"Who? Little Man?" Magic asks for clarification.

"No." Frustration tinges Toga's tone. "Ben."

"Dammit." Magic runs a hand over his head. "I'll go fill Snow in."

With that, he disappears to find their president. Toga shifts to face me and cups my cheeks.

"I'm sorry."

I lean into his touch. "What are you sorry for? This is my fault."

"It's not your fault, Kid. And I'm sorry I fell for it."

"No apology necessary. We all fell for it."

"There's something else I'm sorry for."

"Okay." I drag out the word.

"I'm sorry for not responding earlier, when you told me you loved me."

"Oh." My heart sinks, certain he's going to reject me. "It's okay. I don't want you to say something you don't mean or aren't ready to—"

"I love you too, Fallon. So goddamn much."

Toga's lips crash into mine, and the kiss snaps a bunch of pieces into place. My heart, my soul. I feel whole for the first time in my life.

All of that comes to a screeching halt when my cell phone rings. Toga groans but nods for me to answer it.

"Put it on speaker," he instructs.

I do and when my father's voice comes through the line, all of those perfectly aligned pieces shift.

"I may not have taught you a lot but start taking notes. Because *this*, daughter of mine, is how you fight a war."

CHAPTER 18

TOGA

The sun is bright outside the kitchen window as I finish loading the breakfast dishes into the dishwasher. The sound of Fallon's voice on a conference call is quiet and soothing in the background.

A week has passed since the night Ben created chaos on the compound, and there's been no further communication. I refuse to let my guard down though because he's not done. This is nowhere close to over.

"Sounds like you've got everything under control. We open our doors in just over two weeks. Hopefully, I can get there. In the meantime, I appreciate all that you're doing. And I know our clients will too."

After closing the dishwasher and hitting the start button, I dry my hands on a towel and turn in time to see Fallon enter the kitchen.

"How are things at Source of Love?"

"Great," she responds with false positivity. The way her face falls gives her away.

"Then why do you look like someone just took the last glazed donut from the box?"

124

"The Board of Directors, as well as all the staff, have everything under control. Things seem to be running smoothly and they're able to handle anything that comes up. They're sticking to the budget and are just as excited as I am to open our door. It's just..."

It hits me at this moment just how hard it is for her to follow her dream when it's in another state.

"They're doing it without you," I finish for her.

"Exactly." Fallon pulls out a chair at the table and sits. "They don't need me. The only thing Source of Love needs from me is my money. The rest? They've got it."

"Trust me, they need you. That non-profit is *your* vision, *your* passion, *your* life's work. It doesn't exist without *you*. Don't lose sight of that."

"I'm trying not to."

"I heard you tell them you're going to try to get there for the opening. Is that what you want?"

"Of course it is." She reaches for my hand after I sit down. "Don't get me wrong, Toga, I understand why I'm here and why that might not be possible. But it doesn't mean I have to like it."

"So is that your plan? Stay here only as long as you have to and then just go back to California, back to your old life?"

Irrational anger courses through me. I knew that had to cross her mind at some point, but I thought we were building something here, something together. Maybe I was wrong.

"I don't know, Toga. I can't just walk away forever from everything I've built. But I don't want to walk away from you either. I don't know what the right answer is."

I shoot up from the chair, anger and fear winning out over logic and rational thought. "The right answer is to stay here, with me. The right answer is you want to build a life with me, even if it means compromising on a few things, like where you chase your dream."

Fallon's face reddens, and I know I've crossed a line. It's not fair to ask her to compromise when I know full well, she'd be the one doing all the adjusting. I can't leave... my club, my family is here. Source of Love can exist anywhere, as long as she's there.

"Don't you have some club business to take care of today?" she asks, her tone even.

"There's always club business." I snap my fingers. "Oh, wait. It's not about that. You're running. The second it gets hard, you shut down."

"You would know all about that, wouldn't you?"

Fallon storms off, toward the bedroom. When the door slams shut, I swear I feel the entire house shake. Not wanting to be here, I stomp to the living room, grab my cut, and out the door I go. I get on my Harley and ride, with no destination in mind. I make it all the way to the gate before turning around and heading to the one place I know I'll find someone in my corner.

How did things go this badly? I went from supporting her to throwing any chance of a future down the drain with my insecurities. Not exactly how I pictured the day going.

I pull up in front of Magic's house and see him sitting on the top porch step. A joint dangles from his fingers and smoke curls from his lips.

"What's up, brother?"

I cut the engine and join him. "Not a fucking thing."

He hands me the joint. "Bullshit. We're not supposed to meet for another hour and you're never early. So, spill."

"I fucked up, man." I pass him the joint and rest my elbows on my updrawn knees. Raking my hands through my hair, I try to think about how to explain this to him. He's the last person I'd take relationship advice from, but he's my best friend and a man I know I can trust.

"Aw, shit, what'd you do?"

"Can I just tell you that I may need a place to sleep tonight and leave it at that?"

"Not a chance."

I heave a sigh. "Fine. I pissed Fallon off."

"I could've figured that out all on my own. I want details." He grins. "And you want to give them to me or you wouldn't be here."

"I may or may not have yelled at her for not giving me the answer I wanted when I asked her if she wanted to move back to California."

"Wait, she wants to move back? You guys love each other, she can't leave."

"Apparently, it's not as simple as that. She wants to follow through on Source of Love and do what she feels she was meant to do. But she also doesn't want to leave me."

Magic throws his head back and laughs.

"What the hell's so funny?"

When he sobers, he looks me dead in the eye. "You, brother, are what's so funny."

"I fail to see the humor."

"Who says those two things are mutually exclusive? She can follow her dreams and still be with you. What's to stop her from opening Source of Love, as planned, and then expanding it to Denver? Think outside the box, dude."

"I can't ask her to start over. Not only isn't that fair, but damn, it's expensive. It'd take another huge chunk of the money her mother left her."

"Have you considered putting it before the club, seeing if the non-profit is something we could all get behind? Because I gotta tell ya, what she's doing? Seems like it's right in line with what we do for the community. You might find that Satan's Legacy would cover the cost, or at least some of it."

"You're talking like it's a done deal, Magic. It's not. It takes time and planning. Not only that, but I'm guessing a whole lotta convincing when it comes to some of the members."

"You'd be surprised, brother."

A thought strikes me. "What have you done?"

"Let's just say, I'm not the only one who's had this thought."

"Jesus, does everyone just talk behind my back and plan shit out for me?"

"No. But we *do* have your back, and by extension, Fallon's." Magic stands and stares down at me. "Have you ever considered that you aren't the only one who'd love to see her stay?"

He takes the few steps to the front door but pauses. "If you don't believe me, talk to Laney. She'll tell ya. Besides, she's really who you should be going to for relationship advice."

"Oh really? You do that a lot, do you? Go to her for relationship advice?"

"Sure. She knows her stuff."

"Magic, you don't do relationships."

"I get around."

"See, that's just it. Getting around isn't the same thing at all. I hope to God Laney's told you that."

"She may have said something to that effect."

I stand and reach out to shake Magic's hand. "Thanks, man. I appreciate ya."

"You're welcome. But seriously, go see Laney. I may have helped with one thing, but when it comes to what you're gonna have to do to smooth things over with Fallon, I'm clueless."

"Right. I'll go do that now and meet you back here in time to go take care of that sorry excuse for a drug runner."

I make my way to my Harley and then ride to Laney's. Turns out, she agrees with Magic. And I am as big of an idiot as I acted this morning.

CHAPTER 19

FALLON

Hugging the pillow to my chest, I stare at the clock on the wall. It's a little after nine, and Toga isn't home yet. I try to keep my worries at bay, but it's damn near impossible. When I stormed away from him this morning, I didn't for a second think he wouldn't come home. He's almost always home by this time.

I think back over our argument and wonder where the conversation went wrong. Yes, I could have said things differently, but he could have listened without flying off the handle and making assumptions. I want to be with Toga, to build a future with him, but I need more than that. I'm not going to be the little woman who sits in the corner and stays quiet. I'm not that person who relies on others for my own happiness. Either he's on board with that or he's not.

A knock at the door startles me, and I set the pillow on the couch to go open the door.

"Who is it?" I call out, remembering that I'm not supposed to let anyone in who I don't know.

"It's Laney, honey."

I frantically open the door, concern for Toga fueling my every move.

"Is he okay? Where is he? Why isn't he back yet?"

Laney reaches for my arm and urges me inside so she can shut and lock the door. "Slow down, honey. Toga's fine."

"Then why isn't he home? He always comes home, but not today. Not on the day we fight."

"That's actually what I'm here about." She stretches her arm to indicate the kitchen. "Got anything to drink in there?"

I give my head a shake and try to ground myself. "Yes, of course. Sorry."

We proceed to the kitchen, and I pour us both a whiskey neat. We stand at the end of the peninsula, sipping on our drinks until they're gone. When I can't stand it anymore, I break the silence.

"You said you were here about Toga?"

"Yes, right." Laney lifts her glass, silently asking for more, and while I pour it, she continues. "Toga came to see me this morning, after going to Magic, of course. Surprisingly, Magic gave him some pretty good advice." She takes a sip of her fresh drink. "Anyway, Toga's an idiot and I told him as much. You both are so set in your ways that you're failing to look at the bigger picture."

"What do you mean? All I did was tell him that I wanted to have my non-profit *and* him, but that I didn't know how to make that happen."

"From what I hear, it was a little more explosive than that." When I open my mouth to protest, she holds a hand up to stop me. "Forget that. It doesn't matter. What matters is what you're going to do to make it right."

"Me?" I cry in outrage. "What about him? That argument wasn't one-sided."

"I know that. And I've already told him what he needs to do." She leans across the counter and winks. "Brace yourself for some heavy groveling and make-up sex." She waves her hand dismissively. "Now I want to tell you a few things."

The mention of make-up sex temporarily derails my thoughts, but when my insides start to heat up at a mental image of him naked, I force myself to refocus.

"Go ahead. Tell me what you came to say."

"When he comes home, you need to hear him out, listen to everything he's saying. And quite frankly, everything he's not saying. Because he's a guy and bound to fuck the words up."

"I can do that. But he needs to listen to me, too."

"Yeah, he does. And he will."

"Okay. Anything else?"

"Always."

She downs the rest of her drink and holds her glass out for another.

"Should you really be drinking so much? Don't you have Shiloh at home?"

"First of all, don't question my drinking habits." She wiggles her glass at me. "Second of all, Shiloh is at his uncle's house. We do a lot of sleepovers. I'd never leave him home alone, especially just to drink."

I pour her a third whiskey neat and realize I've just been put in my place. Laney may be my friend, and she's Toga's family, but she's still the club princess and not to be questioned.

"Right. Won't happen again," I assure her. "Please, continue."

"I don't really know how you're going to react to the rest, so..." She downs the third drink, so I pour her another. "Thanks. Anyway, I thought you should know exactly where Toga's at."

"No, no. That's okay. I know I'm not privy to club business."

"That's just it, this club business is about you." She waves her hand. "Besides, I got the okay from Snow to tell you."

"What is it?"

"You have to promise not to tell Toga. Because he's going to come in here at some point and be damn proud of himself for coming up with a solution. I'm only telling you because I want you to have time to process the info and not react out of emotion when he tells you."

"Damn, Laney, what the hell is it?"

I sip on my own drink while she talks.

"Toga and the guys are in church, discussing the future of Source of Love. Satan's Legacy is very interested in having you open an identical non-profit here in Denver, with them footing the bill as far as start-up costs."

Whiskey flies from my mouth and hits her in the face. My eyes widen in horror, but she laughs it off.

"What?! They can't do that. I can't let them do that. This is my project, and no one else is responsible for it but me. Besides, what if it's a bust? What if I fail with the one in California?" I frantically shake my head. "No. Absolutely not."

"I told them you'd say that." She covers my hand with hers. "There's more, honey."

"What the hell?"

"You can say no. You will always have a say in what happens with Source of Love. It is yours, after all. But what you need to know is Satan's Legacy will be opening a non-profit, with or without your support and expertise, regardless of what it's called. Wouldn't it be better if you're here to run it, to make sure it falls in line exactly with your vision? Furthermore, wouldn't it be better for you and Toga? I, for one, think the two of you deserve this chance. You both deserve to be happy."

"Well, yeah, I do too."

"Then take the leap, honey," she encourages. "When he tells you all about 'his plan'..." Laney actually uses air quotes. "... say yes and jump in with both feet. If it doesn't work, you can both walk away knowing you tried everything. But if it works? Damn, wouldn't that be something?"

There are no words. What Laney is saying makes sense. I'm a little surprised I didn't think of it earlier. But is this really what Toga wants? I know I need to ask him that. And really listen to what he has to say.

"Thanks, Laney."

"You're welcome." Laney walks out of the kitchen, toward the front door. "I'm gonna head home. I'm not sure what time Toga will be home, but he will be. In the meantime, try to get some sleep. I have a feeling you've got a lot of work ahead of you."

She disappears into the night, and I lock the door behind her. Rather than return to my place on the couch, I head for bed. I don't know if I'll sleep or not, but I can think there as well as anywhere.

In the bedroom I take my clothes off and let them fall to the floor. Normally, I'd put them in the hamper, but I'm kinda hoping Toga will see them when he gets home.

Him spotting my discarded clothing may lead to that make-up sex Laney mentioned.

CHAPTER 20
TOGA

Unlocking the door, I'm careful not to make too much noise. My hope is that Fallon is sleeping. There's so much I want to talk to her about, apologies I need to make, but none of that needs to happen at two o'clock in the morning.

After depositing my keys on the side table, I make my way to the bedroom, careful not to step on the floorboards that creak. With each step I take, the bandage on my side pulls at my skin, and pain radiates from behind it. But I ignore it.

I open the door, and the light on her nightstand glows. Her back is toward me, so I can't tell if she's awake or not. My eyes trained on the floor, I make my way across the room, toward the mattress and that's when I see her clothes.

Hint? Or just exhaustion?

I strip my own clothes off and let them pile with Fallon's. Pulling the covers back, I crawl under and scoot closer to her, careful of my wound. When I press my front to her back, she pushes back against me, and I know she's awake.

"What time is it?" she asks, her voice sleepy.

"A little after two." I wrap my arm around her midsection. "Go back to sleep."

"I wasn't sleeping."

"Oh."

Fallon rolls over so she's facing me and rests her hand just above my hip. I wince at the contact, and she notices. Boy, does she notice. She shoots into a sitting position and yanks the blanket off of me. When she spots the bandage, which no doubt has blood seeping through, she gasps.

"What the hell happened? Are you okay? Do you need to go to the hospital?"

Fallon jumps out of bed and reaches for her clothes to start getting dressed. I sit up and reach for her arm to stop her.

"Fallon, baby, slow down," I urge. "I'm fine. Just a little cut."

"Just a little cut, my ass. That's a pretty big bandage for 'just a little cut'. Were you stabbed? What happened?"

"Yes, I took a knife to my side. Nothing I haven't felt before and nothing some stitches and pain meds can't fix. Both of which I got from Carnie."

"Carnie isn't a real doctor! A hospital would surely do a better job."

"Carnie is as good as any doctor, and with him, there's no paper trail. Seriously, I'll be fine."

Fallon flops down on the bed next to me. "Can you tell me exactly what happened or is that need to know?"

"Is it a deal breaker if I can't tell you?"

She folds her arms across her naked breasts, which only serves to push them up and beg to be touched.

"No, it's not a deal breaker."

"Then it's need to know. I can tell you it's a knife wound, but it's not serious. I can tell you that it isn't the first time I've been stabbed and it likely won't be the last. But I am okay." I pull the bandage away from my skin. "See, all good."

Fallon gently touches the skin around the giant slash. It's a good few inches long but not very deep. After a moment, she bends down to get her clothes and starts to put her tank top on.

"What are you doing?" I ask, yanking the shirt out of her hands.

"Well, you're in no condition for make-up sex..."

"Says who?"

"Uh, that knife wound."

"Baby, no injury could ever stop me from wanting you. Slow me down? Maybe, but I doubt it. Change how we do things for a day or two? Sure. But keep me from fucking you? Never."

"So you want to have sex? Even when you're in pain?"

I grab her hand and wrap her fingers around my cock. "You tell me."

Fallon grins, as big as the Cheshire Cat. She removes her hand so she can lift mine to her mouth, where she proceeds to suck on each of my fingers, swirling her tongue around them. It wouldn't take long for me to come like a fucking teenager, so I stop her.

"Not like that."

"Then show me what you want," she taunts.

"Get on the bed, on your knees," I command.

She scrambles to do as she's told, and I stand so I can take her from behind. This is the best way we can both chase our pleasure without it causing too much damage.

I grab ahold of Fallon's hips and lift her ass in the air so I can line up with her entrance. I swipe a finger through her folds, making sure she's ready for me. Because this isn't going to be slow or easy.

I thrust into Fallon's wet heat, and she immediately clamps down on my cock. Moans fill the room as her hands fist in the sheets. She pushes back with each forward motion of my body, and I fill her completely. Maybe it's the 'make-up' part of the sex, or maybe it's just her, but I'm not going to last long at all. I can already feel tingles racing up my back, but I can't let go until she comes.

"Touch yourself, baby. Come with me."

Fallon reaches down and rubs fast circles around her clit. Her legs begin to shake, and her pussy starts to spasm.

"That's it."

I increase my pace, ignoring the twinge of pain in my side. Within seconds, her arm starts to give out and she groans with her release. As she clamps down on me, my dick pulses inside her and we soar together.

Afterward, she collapses onto the mattress, and I do the same but quickly roll to the side so I don't crush her.

"Sorry," I say, unnecessarily. "That wasn't nearly as long as I was hoping."

"Still the best sex ever," she assures me.

I pull her into my arms and drag her toward the head of the bed so we can rest on the pillows and get comfortable.

"I hope you know I wasn't planning or expecting that when I got home."

"I know, Toga." She wraps her arm around my waist, careful not to touch my wound. "I hope you know that the clothes were just a hint, not an expectation."

"I do." I give her a peck on the lips. "You know we need to talk, right?"

"Yep."

"It can wait until—"

"No, Toga, it can't wait," she says and sits up. "I don't want another minute to go by where we're not on the same page."

I scoot into a sitting position and lean back against the headboard next to her. "I agree."

"Good, I'll start." She glances at me out of the corner of her eye. "If that's okay?"

"Of course."

Fallon takes a deep breath and blows it out slowly. "I'm sorry for the way I handled the situation. I think you know I meant what I said, but there were better ways I could have said it, and for that, I'm sorry."

"I'm sorry I handled it the way I did too. All I heard was you wanted to go back to California and I kinda freaked. I don't want to be without you, Fallon. I love you. But I realize that part of loving someone is letting them go if that's what makes them happy."

"Is that really what you think? That leaving you would make me happy?"

I shrug. "I don't know."

"Let's get one thing straight," she says.

She turns to face me and sits cross-legged. It's hard to focus with her pussy on full display, but I manage. This is too important to screw up because of my overly active penis.

"I love you, and I want to be with you, make a life with you. Nothing will ever change that. Got it?"

"Got it."

"But I also want to move forward with Source of Love. I want to see it become what I know it can be. I don't want to give up on my dream because of a man, even *if* that man is the most amazing man I've ever known."

"I don't want to see you give up on anything. I want everything you want." It's now or never. She's either going to hate my idea or love it. "And I think I have a solution."

Fallon tilts her head. "Oh yeah, what's that?" There's skepticism in her voice, but not as much as I expected.

"I think you should keep moving forward with Source of Love, get it up and running and see it through all of that. If that means that we travel back and forth between California and Colorado to make it happen, then so be it."

"Okay, that sounds good. Definitely an option, one I could live with."

"There's more."

"Go on."

"Once the original Source of Love—"

"Original?"

"Just hear me out." She nods for me to continue. "Once the original is up and running, we make sure there's an amazing team in place to keep it going. All of which you would oversee... from here. And while you're overseeing that location, we start a Source of Love right here in Denver."

Her eyes light up for a moment before her face falls. "That's great, in theory, Toga. But what about the financial aspect? Source of Love and everything that went into just getting it started wasn't a small chunk of change. I still have a few million left of my mother's money, but I want to set some aside for kids and college funds and travel and retirement. I want to have a life, hopefully with you, outside of work."

"I thought you'd worry about that, so I did a thing."

"You did a thing?"

I nod. "I met with all voting members of Satan's Legacy tonight, and it was a unanimous yes to fund any and all things Source of Love in Denver."

"I can't let you, or them, do that," she argues.

"Why not?"

"Because this is my passion, not yours and certainly not theirs."

"That's where you're wrong, Fallon. *You* are my passion, and that means if *you're* passionate about it then so am I. As far as the club goes, I told you we do a lot for the community. This is one more thing we can do, and it'll mean something. We'll be able to provide more than just protection and fun events. We all want to do this. Trust me, if there were a single member against it, the offer wouldn't be on the table."

Fallon stares past me for a few minutes, no doubt weighing her options. I've laid it all out for her. What happens from this moment forward is up to her.

"If I say yes to this, I need to know this isn't just some short-term fix because we got into a fight."

"I'm in this with you for as long as you want me to be. I would love it if we could live a thousand lifetimes together, but I'll take the one if that's all I can get."

"Does that mean you want everything with me? Marriage, kids, maybe a dog or two?"

"I'll even throw in a white picket fence if you want."

She nods.

"Then I'm in. I'm going to leap with you and see where we land... together."

CHAPTER 21
FALLON

My eyes flutter open as a clap of thunder rattles the windows. A flash of lightning comes between the slats on the blinds. I roll over and notice the empty space next to me. Sitting up, I rub the sleep from my eyes and get out of bed. I grab my robe from the chair against the wall and throw it on before going in search of Toga.

Not that it'll be hard to find him. His morning routine is nothing if not predictable. I head out to the living room and see him in his usual spot on the couch, laptop balanced on his legs and coffee in hand.

"Anything?"

Rather than wait for his standard head shake, I make my way to the kitchen to get coffee.

"She got married again."

I whirl around before I can take my first sip. "What?" I rush to sit next to him. "When? To who?"

He turns the laptop so I can see the screen. On it is a photo from a news article, or more accurately, a gossip rag. The headline jumps out at me, and I cringe.

Gold Digger or Woman in Love?

"At least Mom is consistent, huh?"

Toga hands me the laptop and stands up to pace. I skim through the poorly edited article and see that Margaret Hart—I guess she never changed her name—married Hamilton Nash yesterday during a 'short, but meaningful' ceremony at a small Catholic church in Connecticut. Their courtship, according to the writer, was very private, but then he goes on to assure his readers that it was 'the stuff fairytales are made of'.

It takes everything in me not to puke. Clearly this person doesn't like Margaret and feels she's using this Hamilton guy for his money, but he doesn't hesitate to wax poetic about the things he doesn't find abhorrent. When I get toward the end of the article, I focus on the last paragraph, which is another bashing of Margaret and her motives.

"Did you read all of this?"

"Yep."

"Even the last paragraph?"

"Yep."

"Thoughts?"

"Probably the same as you. My mother has been supporting your father over the last few months with money from the new man in her life." He laughs humorously. "Oh wait, not just the new man in her life, my new goddamn step-dad."

He hurls his mug at the wall, and it shatters, sending coffee and ceramic pieces flying. The noise causes me to flinch, but I don't let Toga see the reaction. I can't blame him for how he's feeling. He may not be close to his mom, but this is betrayal on a whole new level. Margaret is very aware of how Ben works.

That's why she left in the first place. Why do something that's guaranteed to pull her back into his web of lies and deception? Why help hurt other people you supposedly care about?

"Yeah, that's the gist I got too."

"I know you're upset and hurt, but we'll get through this, Toga." I set the laptop on the table and go to him. I grab his arm, forcing him to stop pacing. "Have you talked to her at all since you left?"

He shakes his head.

"Maybe now would be a good time to reach out."

I know it's a suggestion he doesn't want to hear. But it seems to be our only option at this point. He needs to call her and see if she'll talk to him, maybe tell him why, or how. And if she chooses not to open up, then at least we know where to focus our energy when it comes to taking my dad down. Impede the cash flow, impede his ability to keep coming after me.

"I have nothing to say to her. The moment my father died, she quit being a mother to me. She clinched that when she chose Ben over me. Now she's not only helping Ben, whose hurting you, but she got married and didn't even fucking tell me."

I don't bother questioning how she was supposed to get in touch with him because it doesn't matter at this point.

"And despite all that, she can get us a step closer to my father. I'm not saying call her and bond or anything. Call her and use her for information."

Toga narrows his eyes at me. "Why do you have to make so much sense?"

"Because I'm smart like that." I pat him on the back like a coach would. "C'mon, you got this."

Toga takes a deep breath and then takes his cell out of

his pocket. He stabs his finger at the screen several times, and before I know it, the line is ringing.

"You don't have to put it on speaker," I tell him.

"I know."

"Hello?"

That voice. I'll never forget it. It belongs to the woman who tried to protect me years ago, even if she wouldn't protect her own son. Now all I hear is a woman whom life has beaten down and turned into a traitor. And she's a newlywed for Christ's sake. She should be fucking happy.

"Hello, who is this?"

"Hello, Mom," Toga finally says.

She gasps but quickly composes herself. "David?"

"Do you have other children I don't know about?"

"Of course not. It's just been so long since I've heard your voice." There are tears in her voice, like her throat is clogging up, but I don't buy it. "Oh, David, I have some wonderful news."

"You're married. I know." Toga thrusts a hand through his hair. "I didn't call to congratulate you."

"No? Oh, well, that's okay, I suppose. If you don't mind me asking then, why did you call?"

"A friend thought it would be a good idea."

"A friend? How thoughtful. You must thank them for me. It's been too long since we last spoke."

"Since we last... Are you fucking kidding me? We didn't speak, Mom. We argued about whether or not what I was doing was fair. You begged me to stay in a toxic and violent situation. And then you watched me walk out the door. I'd hardly call that a conversation." Toga takes a deep breath and turns the conversation back to the matter at hand. "But again, not why I called."

"Oh, yes. The friend. It was always so hard for you to make friends. I'm glad that seems to have changed."

"Oh my God, do you even hear yourself? I have friends, more than any one man deserves. I have family and people who give a shit about me. Why is that so hard for you to believe?"

"It's not, dear. So, who is this friend that urged you to call. Maybe I could meet him some day."

"You already know her. Or maybe you've forgotten. You forgot about me easily enough." Toga nods at me to say something.

"Hi Margaret."

Another gasp. The theatrics are strong with this one.

"Fallon? Is that you?"

"Yep, it's me."

"Oh goodness. I haven't heard from you in almost a year. I was starting to worry. But it seems you're doing well, and it makes me so happy that the two of you found each other again."

"Yeah, I found her. In a hospital bed, clinging to life, because your ex-husband tried to kill her."

"No, that can't be right," Margaret protests.

"From what I can gather, you may be helping to end her life more than you think. Or maybe you know all about Ben's plans and you just don't care. That sounds more accurate to me. So, *Mom*, which is it? Are you helping or are you a victim yourself?"

Margaret pauses so long that it doesn't matter what she says. She's not a victim, and there's no way she'll convince Toga otherwise.

"I simply don't know what you're talking about. All I've done was give Ben a few bucks here and there. I feel so bad for him, struggling like he is."

"Only he's not struggling. Because you're giving him way more than a few bucks. A few hundred thousand maybe. I know he's getting money from loan sharks, but you? Even I didn't see that coming. What'd you do Mom? Slip him a few thousand here and there, along with an address or phone number? I'm sure he gave you some sob story or another about Fallon and how he just had to find her."

"Of course he had to find her," she cries. "She's his daughter. Besides, how else was he supposed to tell her about his cancer diagnosis?"

"You can't be that dumb," Toga accuses.

"That's no way to talk to your mother," Margaret snaps.

"If I were talking to my mother, I'd agree with you. As far as I'm concerned, my mother died the moment my father did. Now, you're going to answer a few questions for me, and then we're never going to speak again. I will make sure no one comes after you, even though that goes against my better judgment. That's where you and I are different. I actually give a rat's ass about blood. So, answer the questions, and I leave you alone. Don't answer, and I will hunt you down and watch as my family ends your life. The choice is yours."

"What are your questions?" Margaret's tone is no longer soft or flighty. It's harsh and full of anger.

"When is the next time you're supposed to talk to or see Ben?"

"He's supposed to call me next week with a location in California for me to meet him the following week."

"What phone number does he use when he calls you?" Margaret provides the number, and Toga writes it down. "Do you hand off the money in person or transfer it?"

"Both."

"I need the account numbers you transfer money to for him." Again, she rattles off numbers, and he writes them down.

Toga is quiet for so long I half expect Margaret to just hang up. I would if I were her.

"Is that all?" she finally asks after a few more minutes.

Toga locks eyes with me, and there's a sheen to them I'm not used to seeing. He can play the tough guy role all he wants, but at his core, he's just a man. One with feelings that sometimes get hurt.

"No, that's not all." Toga clears his throat. "Are you happy?"

"As much as I deserve to be."

With that, Margaret disconnects the call.

"I think that was the first honest thing she said during that entire phone call," I remark, not knowing what else to say.

Toga nods even as a tear slips down his cheek, followed by another and then another. His shoulders shake, and he hangs his head. It's a sight to see him like this. Big, strong, tattooed man with a mohawk, bawling like a baby.

We're standing on opposite sides of the peninsula, so I jump up and crawl across it. I sit on my ass and pull him between my legs so I can hold him while he cries. Rubbing circles over his back, I offer comfort simply by being here.

When his tears subside, he wipes his nose on the sleeve of his shirt and stares at me with pain in his eyes.

"I wasn't expecting that," he admits.

"I know you weren't."

"How is it that the people who are supposed to love us unconditionally end up being the ones who hurt us the most?"

"I wish I knew." I rest my hands on his sides, careful not

to rub his bandage. "But you were right. You've got an amazing family and support system here with Satan's Legacy. And you'll always have me. Always."

Toga kisses my forehead. "I love you, Kid."

"I love you too."

CHAPTER 22
TOGA

"Did you get the hotel booked?"

I nod at Brady while Carnie continues to check my stitches. We're in church, but things have been so hectic, it's the only time either of us have. And since Fallon and I can't keep our hands off each other, there's bound to be a few that need fixed. The others are focused on what Carnie is doing, but they're just as focused on the conversation as I am.

"What about the rental car?"

"I got it all done. Fake names and all."

"I know you think it's counterproductive to use different names, but we don't want to make it too easy for Ben. Otherwise, he'll spy the trap," Snow reminds me.

He and I have had the same argument several times in the last week, and since he's the president, I'll defer to him. Doesn't mean I have to like it.

"I get it," I tell him. "I just think we're putting a bigger target on our backs than is necessary."

"All of this has already been discussed so let's table it for now." Duck's voice booms through the room. He's a goofy guy but a great VP. And when he wants something to happen, like tabling a discussion, he has no problem letting you know.

"Brady, did you manage to get the trap and trace on the phone number I gave you?"

"Sure did. I also linked into the bank account you got from your... from Margaret."

"Good. I don't want to drain it yet, but the second Ben's been taken out, take the money."

"I've got everything set up and ready to go."

"Toga, are you sure you don't want any of us to go to the opening in Cali?" Snow asks. "I don't want you and Fallon to be alone with a psychopath after you."

"We'll be fine. I'm not gonna let anything happen to her."

"It's not just her I'm worried about. Who's going to watch your back while you're watching Fallon's?" Snow looks around the room, and his eyes land on Magic. "You go with them."

"Now wait a damn minute." I move away from Carnie just as he latches onto a stitch with a pair of tweezers. "Motherfucker! That hurt."

"Don't move if you don't want it to hurt." Carnie shrugs and shifts closer to me to finish fixing the stitch.

I glare at Snow. "I told you before, and I'll tell you again... I don't need a goddamn babysitter."

"Maybe not, but you're getting one anyway," Snow snarls. "If you would have approached this a little differently and given me a logical reason for not needing someone else there, maybe I'd have listened. As it stands, you're shit out of luck, brother."

"See, Toga. I told you to get a grip on that temper of yours," Magic says, throwing gasoline on the fire.

"Don't start with me, asshole."

"Both of you, shut up," Duck snaps as he stands from his chair. "Your president has told you what's going to happen, and you either follow along or get the fuck out."

"No one's going anywhere, Duck," Snow says. "They're both gonna cooperate." He pins Magic and then me with his stare. "Aren't ya boys?"

I can feel the others staring, wondering what's going to happen. Magic and I speak simultaneously.

"Yes, sir."

"Good. Now, anything else we need to discuss?"

"Yeah. Fallon spoke with her accountant and gave him the go ahead to talk finances with Spark." I glance at our Treasurer. "She gave him your cell number, Spark, so watch for his call."

"Will do."

"Also, Fallon asked if she could have a month to work with the California Source of Love before she dives in here. I think she just wants to make sure that any kinks that might come up are worked through so they aren't repeated here."

"Anyone have a problem with that?" Snow asks. A chorus of 'no's echo throughout the room. "Tell her that's fine. Oh, and tell her that she can always come to any of us about this project. It doesn't always have to go through you."

"Appreciate that. I'll let her know. I think right now there's just a lot going on and it's easier to talk to me. We do a lot of our talking in bed."

"Wait," Duck interjects. "You mean to tell me that you waste time in bed talking? Have we taught you nothing?"

"Fuck off," I say with a laugh.

"Just saying, that's messed up, bro."

"Yeah, well, I happen to like it. Wait until you find a woman you love. You just might like it too."

"Jesus, do we have to get all up in our feelings?" Dip complains.

"No, we don't. Anything else before I adjourn?" Snow asks one more time.

When no one says anything, he dismisses us. I stay behind to let Carnie finish the last few stitches. Apparently, the man felt the need to replace them all. Magic stays behind as well.

"You know Snow knows you can handle yourself, right?" Magic asks when the room is quiet.

"Ya sure about that? Because lately it seems he doesn't trust me all that much."

Magic glances at Carnie, who seems to be in his own little doctor world.

"You're forgetting that Snow just went through what you're going through... the whole falling in love thing. Sending me with you is his way of telling you he understands and wouldn't blame you one bit if your head wasn't completely in the game. He's showing you that he gets it."

"You should listen to Magic," Carnie pipes in, startling both Magic and me. "Boy knows what he's talking about."

Magic and I exchange a look.

"Just 'cause I look dumb don't mean I ain't payin' attention," he continues and wags his finger at us. "Someone's always payin' attention." He finishes up with the last stitch and starts putting his stuff into his bag. "There, all fixed. Now, don't go tryin' none of that porno shit in the bedroom for a while. Ya gotta give those a chance to heal."

"Thanks, Carnie," I say. "Oh, and uh... can we—"

"I ain't fixin' to tell no one what I overheard. Unlike you, I don't go flappin' my gums every chance I get."

"Right. Thanks."

Carnie leaves the room with no more words of wisdom, leaving Magic and I to consider what he said.

"He's right, ya know?" Magic says. "I do know what I'm talking about."

"I already agreed to let you tag along," I remind him.

"I know." Magic shrugs. "But it isn't often I get to be the smarter one in a room. Let me have my moment."

"Fine, asshole. Have your fucking moment."

CHAPTER 23
FALLON

"Quit kicking the seat, fucker."

We're four hours into our trip back to California, having left at three this morning, and Toga and Magic have been arguing like little kids.

"I'm trying to get comfortable. It's not exactly roomy in the back of this thing."

'This thing' he's referring to is the rental car. We decided against taking the truck, just so we don't have a target on our backs while we're driving. It won't ensure that, but it should help. And it's not like we're in a clown car or anything. Carnie doesn't let anyone drive that.

Seriously, though, it's a Jeep Cherokee with plenty of space for the average person to stretch out. Magic is just anything but average. Unfortunately for him, Toga is less average than he is, which means Magic is stuck in the back.

"Fallon, why can't you sit back here? You're the smallest one," Magic whines.

"Because you insisted on flipping a coin back at the

compound, saying you wanted things to be fair," I remind him. "You lost. Suck it up buttercup."

Magic huffs out a breath but shuts up. It's about damn time.

"You getting excited?" Toga asks me. "Only two more days until Source of Love opens."

"Excited, terrified. You name it, I'm feeling it."

"It's gonna be great. With you at the helm, it couldn't be anything else."

I turn to smile at Magic. "Thanks. I appreciate that."

"He's right," Toga agrees as he reaches across the seat and links his fingers with mine. "I'm so damn proud of you."

I squeeze his hand and hold on tight. I want to hold onto this feeling forever, hold onto him.

"What's the schedule for opening day?" Magic asks.

"We open our doors at nine. We've invited agencies across the county, school counselors, hospital social workers, and basically anyone who might refer clients to come check us out. We've also put out several news articles and advertisements about the opening, which invite the general public to come after five in the evening. There'll be staff throughout the building to answer any and all questions. We'll review the process to get services through us, as well as our mission statement. I want people to leave our building and feel comfortable picking up the phone to contact us, to feel like they can come back. Being that we're going to be working with children from abusive homes, as well as the non-offending parent or caregiver, I want everyone to walk away knowing we'll provide not only a safe haven, but a one stop shop, so to speak, of resources and services geared toward that population."

"Wow. That's a lot."

"And it's all stuff you'd know about if you paid attention," Toga accuses.

"Don't start," I implore Toga. "We've got a long drive ahead of us if we're going to get there tonight and I don't intend on spending the day listening to you guys bicker back and forth like children."

"Yes, ma'am," they both say in unison.

"Thank you. Now, if you don't mind, I'm going to take a nap."

I roll my pillow up between my head and the passenger window and shift around until I'm comfortable. I'd love to lay across the seat like I did in the truck, but that's not possible in this thing, so I'll take what I can get.

I hear the two of them talking about their Harley's as I drift off to sleep. It takes longer than I thought it would, which I attribute to my nerves... and the stress of knowing a confrontation with Ben is imminent.

I have no idea how long I sleep but I'm jolted awake by the sound of a song I despise and Toga smacking my leg.

"Fallon, baby, wake up. Your phone's ringing."

I slowly straighten and glance at him. "That can't be my phone." I bend over and dig my cell out of my bag on the floor. When I confirm that it is, indeed, ringing, I freeze.

"Good song," Magic remarks.

"Horrible song," I snap.

"If it's horrible, why is it your ringtone?"

The song ends but I know it's just a matter of time before it starts back up again. That's how my father rolls.

"It's not. Or at least, it's not anymore," I say and then go on to explain. "It's the ringtone I had set up for my dad." I glance at Toga. "On my old phone. I never put it on this phone."

All Nightmare Long by Metallica starts playing again and I cringe.

"Answer it but keep it on speaker."

I tap the 'answer' button and quickly follow with the 'speaker' button. "How did you do that? How did you get into my phone to change my ringtone?" I demand.

"Fallon, Fallon, Fallon. When are you going to learn that I have skills and connections that you simply don't know about?"

"What do you want?"

"I see you and that trash stepson of mine are on your way to California. Oh, and that other guy you're bringing you? Nice touch and very cute how you think the three of you can take me down."

"Fuck you, old man," Toga snarls.

"Oh, David. Still a belligerent asshole I see. You're forgetting I saw you in action not all that long ago. Was on the receiving end no less. And I gotta say, I'm not exactly afraid of you."

"Hey prick," Magic says from the back seat. "Back off now and maybe we'll let you live."

Dad's tone changes immediately. There's no more teasing, no more taunting, just straight up evil.

"We both know you won't do that. So, here's what's going to happen," he begins harshly. "I've clearly proven I can get to Fallon anytime I want. Especially in the next two days since I have her itinerary. I'm willing to be the bigger man and leave the bitch alone. I just need something for my generosity."

"You're not getting Mom's money!" I shriek, tired of his games. "She left it to me because she hated you. If money is what you're after, go back to the loan sharks or Margaret!"

"I'm glad you brought Margaret up. I knew I could

manipulate her, but I wasn't expecting it to be that easy." He pauses for a moment but not long enough for anyone else to speak. "But then she had to go and run her mouth to you, which is forcing my hand. I could have let it go but then you and your goon squad had to go digging around in my bank accounts. Don't think I don't notice this shit."

"Okay, Margaret blabbed, and you're pissed. What's that got to do with me?"

"Well, if you and Toga aren't interested in saving your own asses, I'll have to shift my efforts to Margaret."

Toga yanks the steering wheel to the right and throws the vehicle in park on the side of the highway. His entire demeanor screams murder. His face is red, his muscles are tense, he's wearing a scowl that I worry will never fade. Toga is enraged and if it weren't for the situation causing it, I'd be a little turned on right now.

"I swear to fucking Christ, Ben," he seethes. "If you touch a hair on my mother's head, cause her harm in any way, I'll make your death infinitely more painful than I'm already planning to."

"Oh, David, you misunderstand. I don't want to hurt Margaret. But you're kind of forcing my hand, don't you think?" My father takes a deep breath before continuing. "Bring me the money. It's that simple. Money equals safety and freedom. I think ten million will do the trick."

"Ten million?!" I cry. "I don't have ten million and you know it."

"Maybe not, but if Toga's club can financially back another Source of Love location, I'm sure they can help you out with this. Or maybe they just don't care about you enough to get involved. I wouldn't blame them really. You're not worth a damn. Never have been and never will be. Hell, you couldn't even die right. If you'd died that night, none of us would be in this mess."

Toga snatches the phone from my hand and brings it closer to his face. "Listen to me, Ben, because I'm not going to say it again. You are a waste of a human body. Clearly you're hellbent on following this through. You've been warned that it won't end well for you, but you refuse to accept that. What happens next is up to you. Walk away and, like our man in the back seat said, you might get to live out the rest of your days. Don't walk away and you better be prepared to fight to the death because that's the only way this will end, in death. Your death. I don't give a shit what you decide to do although it would be more satisfying for me if you continued to be reckless." Toga shrugs even though my father can't see him. "I'm genuinely looking forward to seeing what happens next."

Toga ends the call and tosses my cell into my lap. We all sit there quietly, taking in what just happened. My heart is pounding wildly, and I feel like throwing up. How did we get here? How did I go from being the victim of child abuse to being a grown woman who's still having to save herself from the devil?

"So, uh…" Magic is the first to speak. "We're protecting Margaret now?"

Toga whirls around to face him and snarls, "That's what you got out of all of that?"

The fact that Toga doesn't recognize one of Magic's feeble attempts at humor is telling. Shit, even I see it.

I rest my hand on Toga's arm, but he shakes it off. Sighing, I try again. This time he lets my hand remain. "Toga, he's just trying to lighten the mood." I look over my shoulder and glare at Magic. "Even if he is doing a piss poor job of it."

"I may not love my mother, or even like her, but I'll be fucking damned if she gets hurt at the hands of that douchebag." Toga takes a deep breath and holds his for a second before continuing. "I'm not the monster here, he is."

"Sorry, bro. Fallon's right, I didn't mean anything by it." Magic rests his hand on Toga's shoulder. "And you don't have to explain anything to me. I get it. You might hate the woman but at the end of the day, she's still your mom. She's family, like it or not."

"She's not family, she's blood. There's a difference. But yeah, sometimes, under the right circumstances, blood matters. Besides, I refuse to let that man wreak any more havoc than he already has. He doesn't deserve the satisfaction it brings him."

"You're right," I agree. "So, we continue as planned. Get to California, check into the hotel and get a good night's sleep. Tomorrow we'll make sure we have everything we need to carry out the plan, and then go to finalize any last-minute stuff at Source of Love."

Toga nods while I speak, and I can only hope he's really hearing the words coming from my mouth. He starts the Jeep and pulls back out on the highway.

"Toga, brother, we're gonna get him. In less than seventy-two hours he'll be dead. Remember that, keep it in the back of your mind, because right now, your focus needs to be on Fallon and what she needs. At the end of the day, this trip is about her and her accomplishments. Taking Ben out is the added bonus."

Toga's hands clench and unclench around the steering wheel, but minute by minute, he's calming down. By the time we stop for lunch, and thanks to Magic and his incessant need to act like a child, things in the Jeep are back to normal.

The problem with Toga calming down is it seems he transferred all his rage to me. The further we drive, the angrier I become. How dare my father ruin one of the best days of my life? How dare he make everything about him when all the things I've done with my life I've done despite him?

Nerves roll around and ball up with my anger, as does stress and fear. The combination is sickening and exhausting. I rest my head on my pillow with the hope that I can sleep some of the emotions away and as I drift off, happiness and excitement start to filter in.

It's going to be over soon. I get to help take down the villain of my story. And I'm going to enjoy every single second of it.

CHAPTER 24
TOGA

"Holy... Wow, you look..."

Magic smacks me on the arm and nods in the direction of the bathroom. It's opening day at Source of Love, and it's been an hour and a half since she started getting ready. She packed several outfits for the trip, all of which would have looked amazing on her, but this one, with the black skirt, tailored blazer to match, and red silk blouse underneath? Perfection. Oh, and let's not forget the black Louboutin's I bought here before we left Denver, specifically for this occasion.

I close the distance between us and cup the sides of her neck. "Amazing," I finish for him. "You look amazing."

I fuse my lips with hers and we lose ourselves in the kiss.

"No, actually, I was trying to say she looks like a sexy librarian who I'd sneak in after hours to bone," Magic states. Neither of us break our connection. It's not a comment I'd normally let go but Fallon tastes like spearmint toothpaste and sunshine, and I'm not giving that up. "No reaction? Oh... um..." Magic clears his throat. "Okay, guys, this is getting uncomfortable now. You're really not going to come up for air?"

Fallon pulls away from me and smiles. "You're gonna let him get away with that whole sexy librarian thing?"

I shrug. "I'm in a good mood, what can I say?"

"Lucky for him, I guess."

"Seriously, guys, I'm right here."

Both Fallon and I turn to face Magic.

"Oh, geez," Fallon says dramatically. "I didn't even see you there."

"How 'bout I just go so you too can... well, do whatever it is you want to do."

I glance at Fallon, as if looking to her for whether or not we stop him, and she just laughs before glancing at him.

"Magic, we'd love it if you'd stay," she says with a chuckle. "Besides, we don't have time for any fun. We gotta go in a few minutes."

"She's right," I agree. "But for the record, I haven't forgotten that comment."

"Didn't think you would," Magic counters.

I turn to Fallon. "Do you have everything you need for the opening?"

Fallon walks to the dresser and picks up her bag. "Yep. All right here," she says as she slings it over her shoulder and pats it.

"And you, Magic," I say, turning back toward him. "You've got everything for our plan?"

Magic bends and lifts a large duffel off the floor to toss it on the bed. "Yep. All right here."

He starts pulling weapons out. There are several guns, numerous knives, a grenade, a box of matches, rope, zip ties, duct tape, and an IV. Ya know, in case we really want to torture Ben and drag things out. We're prepared for every scenario.

"Do I get any of that?" Fallon asks, her tone a little too giddy. When she sees my forehead scrunch, she clarifies. "Just in case."

I walk to the duffel and grab a knife from the pile inside. I rub my thumb across the blade, as if inspecting it, before handing it to her.

"Will this work?"

Fallon grabs the handle and flips it over and over in her hand. Unexpectedly, she raises it above her head and brings it down to stab the mattress in one smooth stroke.

"Perfect." She grins, but the grin slips when she registers our surprise. Fallon shrugs. "What? I'll pay for it."

"Have I told you lately how much I love you?"

"You have, but don't let that stop you from saying it again."

"I love you."

"Love you too." Fallon's eyes dart between Magic and me. "Shall we go? I don't want to be late."

"Let's go."

It takes a half hour to get to Source of Love due to traffic. Rather than parking in the garage across the street, I pull in the small lot behind the building, where Fallon has designated spaces for employees.

Fallon smooths her hands down her skirt, as if trying to manually iron out any wrinkles created during the drive here.

"You've got this, Kid." I lean across the console and give her a leisurely kiss. "Magic and I will be here the whole time. We've got your back so you can focus on doing what you need to do."

She nods but doesn't look convinced.

"Do you remember what to do if you spot Ben or if you need one of us to get you out of there?" Magic asks.

"If I see Ben, I'll discreetly excuse myself from what I'm doing and move to stand next to the front door. That way, if I have to run for some reason, I've got a clear exit."

"Good, and if you need to be whisked away?"

"I'll call out to my employees and ask if any of them have the number for the copy machine troubleshooting line. That way you'll hear me, and I won't raise suspicion."

"See," Magic says. "You've got this."

Fallon bites her bottom lip. "What if he doesn't show?"

"He will," I assure her. Although I don't know how reassuring it is.

"But if he doesn't?"

"If he doesn't, we have a backup plan. Brady is already tracing Ben's cell and he's on standby if we need him. He's also tracking my mother. We both know Ben isn't just going to let Margaret walk away and hurting her, in his mind, is another way to hurt us."

Fallon nods but still looks apprehensive. "Okay. Good. I just don't want anything to go wrong."

"I can't promise you that it won't. But I can promise you that we have contingency plan after contingency plan. You'll be safe."

Again, Fallon nods, but she doesn't say anything. Instead, she opens the passenger door and steps out. Magic and I follow suit. I watch as she squares her shoulders and walks toward the door with purpose and pride.

Before she opens the door, she takes a deep breath and tips her head back to look at the sky.

"You did your job that night in my apartment, but I need you again, Mom. I need a guardian angel to watch over me. After today, you can rest easy because Toga will be taking over."

Listening to Fallon talk to her mom makes my eyes burn with unshed tears. I've heard the stories, seen the photos and home movies. Fallon's mom loved her like a mother should. She cherished her daughter and protected her to the best of her ability.

I guess there's a part of me that's jealous because I had that once. Only my mom didn't die. And I think it's worse to lose someone even if they're still physically walking around.

But I'm glad Fallon had that. I'm happy that Fallon finds comfort in talking to her mom. The fact that she knows what goodness in people is and hasn't only been on the receiving end of evil... it's made her a better person, a compassionate and kind person. It's made her the woman I love and want to spend the rest of my life with.

"C'mon, you two," Magic says, opening the door for her. "Let's do this."

THREE HOURS later the crowd thins out as it nears lunch time. Fallon had food catered, to ensure there were finger snacks on hand, as well as coffee, water, tea, and juice for any kids. Rather than make her staff run out on their own for lunch, she gives Amanda, her second in command, enough cash to go down the street and grab means for everyone from a local eatery known for their deli sandwiches and hot soups.

I've watched Fallon all morning and learned something important. This is what she was born to do. This is where she's at her best. Now if we can just duplicate it in Denver, we'll be set.

"Seems to be going well," Magic says from beside me.

"You had doubts?" I counter with an ounce of teasing in my tone.

"Where Fallon is concerned? Hell no. I knew Source of Love would be a hit." He grabs my arm and drags me around the counter where he points at the computer. "Have you seen this? She's already got contracts with five local agencies for referrals, as well as requests for her to come speak to several others and brief their staff on Source of Love resources. It's incredible."

I focus my gaze on Fallon, who's standing across the room, talking to a few members of the Board of Directors, completely in her element.

"Yeah, she is."

Magic looks around as if visually sweeping the room. "I did a walk through of the entire building about fifteen minutes ago. Still no sign of Ben."

I lift my glass of water to my lips and take a drink. When I lower it, I say, "He'll be here."

"You keep saying that but last I heard from Brady, Ben's cell hasn't moved from the rental house he's staying in."

"Doesn't mean he's still there."

"No, it doesn't. But..."

"Think about it," I prod. "When would be an ideal time to come here, do the most damage?"

Magic pretends to think it over, but I know he already knows the answer. We've discussed it at length.

"Later, when she officially opens to the general public. When there's a greater possibility of causing her pain because there will be kids here."

"Exactly."

"And I agree, but we talked about that scenario," Magic reminds me, as if I needed reminding. "That would be too easy, and Ben is smart enough, or stupid enough, to not take the easy and predictable route."

"That's right. Sure, he could show up at any time. But my guess is he'll show up at the end, as she's closing up. He knows he has the means, or connections, to walk away from killing her, but a bunch of innocent bystanders, children? No one walks away from that, no matter what their connections are."

"You know he had to think of that, too, and know it's crossed our minds. I guess I'm just wondering if we're completely off track. Are we analyzing things too closely, which makes us vulnerable, makes Fallon vulnerable? Because I have a feeling none of this is going to go down the way we think."

Magic's right. I know he's right. We've focused all our energy on how we think things will go, scrutinizing the way Ben thinks, the way he operates. We've got backup plans for our backup plans. But that still doesn't mean we're prepared. Because when all is said and done, things are gonna go down the way they're gonna go down, no matter what we think and plan for.

"What are you suggesting we do?"

"Nothing." Magic shrugs. "We keep doing what we're doing and be prepared for anything."

I spot Fallon walking toward us, and I nudge Magic with my elbow, silently telling him to keep our conversation between us.

"Keep your guard up," I say to him. "And for fuck's sake, don't scare Fallon with any of this."

"Oooh," Fallon coos when she reaches us. "I heard my name."

I lean across the counter and kiss her cheek. "Of course you did. I was just telling Magic how proud I am of you."

"Is that so?"

"It is," Magic lies. "And I gotta say, he's pretty pathetic about it. On and On. Fallon this, Fallon that. If I had a nickel for every—"

"Enough." Fallon laughs. "I get it. You're tired of hearing my name."

"He's just jealous," I tell her.

"As he should be."

She beams a smile at me before turning to talk to a few staff members. A few minutes later, Amanda walks in with the food. After Magic does a sweep outside to ensure Ben isn't lurking somewhere, we all dig into our lunch.

My ham and turkey sandwich settles in my stomach like a lead balloon. I can't shake loose the thought that we've missed something, that we're not as prepared as we think.

And by extension, that we're letting Fallon down.

CHAPTER 25
FALLON

"You look exhausted."

I lift my gaze from the folder I'm skimming through and glance at Toga. He's leaning against the door jamb of my office, looking equally as tired as I feel.

"I am."

I close the folder and slip it into my bag. I'm taking a lot of stuff back to Denver with me so I can run things from there. We've planned to come back here before we leave, but somehow, mundane work calms me down.

"I think today was a success." He pushes off the door frame and walks behind me. He grips my shoulders and starts to massage. "You're gonna do a lot of good here, Fallon."

It would be so easy to let myself sink into the relaxation he's trying to provide but I can't. Not everything went well today.

"Ben didn't show," I remind him.

Toga's grip tightens for a second before he seems to realize he's hurting me. Rather than continue the massage, he steps to the side and turns so he can lean against the desk while facing me.

"No, he didn't. But the day isn't over."

"That's what I'm afraid of."

Toga spends the next few minutes helping me turn off all the lights and lock up. It's nine o'clock before we leave and head for the hotel.

"I checked in with Brady. Ben's cell is still showing him at the rental house."

"Good, then as long as he stays there, all of this can wait until morning."

Toga and Magic exchange a brief look in the rearview mirror. "I think we need to take him out tonight. It's the safest thing to do."

I rub my temples and don't bother disguising the yawn that escapes. "Please, Toga, can we just leave it for the night? I'm beyond tired. We've waited this long. Hell, *he's* waited this long. What's a few more hours?"

Maybe I'm being horribly naive but the moment I ushered the last staff member out of Source of Love, everything I've done, all my time spent preparing for today, came crashing down on me like a tidal wave. I deserve a break.

"A couple hours," Toga finally agrees. But that's it. We can't wait until daylight. You can get a few hours of sleep. That's all I can give you."

Magic makes a whip sound, and I whirl around to glare at him. "Not now, Magic," I bite out.

He holds his hands up in mock surrender. "Got it. Bad timing."

I return my attention to Toga, who's gripping the steering wheel to the point his knuckles are white. "Thanks. I'll take what I can get."

The rest of the drive is made in silence. When we reach the hotel, the three of us trudge up to our rooms.

"I'm gonna change and then head to the bar downstairs for a drink. Feel free to join me," Magic tells us. "Otherwise, I'll meet you at your room around four. That work?"

"Sounds good."

"Night."

I throw my arms around Magic, and he lifts me in a hug. "Thanks for being there today," I whisper in his ear. I plant a kiss on his cheek, ignoring Toga's protesting groans. "See ya in a few hours."

We go our separate ways, as Magic's room is on the opposite end of the hotel. Toga swipes the keycard and as soon as the lock disengages, he grips the handle and throws open the door.

I enter ahead of him and flip on the light. That's when my heart stops.

"What the hell?" Toga whispers as he draws his weapon.

There, in the middle of the floor, is Margaret. Her cheeks are red and chafed and her eyes are bloodshot. Her wrists and ankles are bound, and she has a gag in her mouth. Toga holds a finger to his lips, and she nods in understanding.

Without a word, he silently makes his way through the suite, making sure Ben isn't around. When he returns to the main room, he sets his gun on one of the tables.

"It's all clear."

I rush forward and drop to my knees next to Margaret. I may not like the woman, but I didn't want her to get hurt in all of this. I remove the gag first and then begin to free her limbs.

"Where is he?" Toga demands the moment Margaret can talk.

"I don't know."

He picks his gun up so quickly, I don't see him coming when he steps up to her side and points it at her head.

"Bullshit. Where is Ben?"

"I told you, I don't know," she cries.

Toga stares at her for a long moment, as if assessing the truthfulness of her statement. He must decide she's being honest because he lowers the gun.

Once I free Margaret, I help her stand before shifting to Toga's side. I don't want there to be any mistake of who's back I have here.

"How long have you been here?" I ask.

"Couple hours, maybe." Margaret shrugs. "I met Ben earlier to hand deliver more money and a burner phone. As soon as he had what he wanted, he tased me. I woke up here."

"Burner phone?" Toga arches a brow.

"Yeah. He said you were tracking his cell and needed a way to move about freely."

"Jesus. So even though Brady was tracking him, we have no idea where he's been."

Toga starts to pace. Back and forth, back and forth, trying to make sense of it all. The problem is it doesn't make sense. None of it. The burner phone, I get. But bringing Margaret here, tying her up? She was helping him so what purpose does that serve. Loose ends, maybe, but something tells me there's more to it than that.

I step closer to Margaret, getting in her space and making it very clear that I expect her to talk.

"Why did you help him in the first place? Because I don't quite believe that you bought into all his bullshit about cancer or whatever else he told you. You know what he's like. So, why?"

Margaret lowers her head into her hands and quietly cries. Finally, something genuine from her. I rest my hand on her shoulder, trying to portray the caring, loving step-daughter.

"Margaret, why help him?" I repeat.

"Because," she wails. "Believe it or not, I love Hamilton. He's a good man and for the first time since David's father died, I finally feel like I've found someone who can make me happy."

The pieces start to click into place. "And Ben threatened that, threatened Hamilton."

It's not a question. Despite Toga's issues with the woman, she's not a bad person. She tried with my father, tried to protect me. But it was impossible.

Toga stops in his tracks and faces her. "Then what was all the shit on the phone the other week? Why not just tell us all this then?"

"Because I was scared. The threats were getting worse. Ben was sending me copies of Hamilton's schedule, proving that he could get to Hamilton any time he wanted."

"So to save your new husband, you sacrificed Fallon? Me?"

Margaret nods and the crying worsens. "I'm not saying I made the right decision. Nor do I expect you to forgive me. I blew it with you a long time ago. But you have to know, I thought I had no other choice."

Regardless of the years that have passed by, Margaret has been stuck in that battered woman mentality. And there's nothing that will let her break free from that, short of killing my father.

Does she deserve that, that freedom? I don't know. But I'm in a very similar boat, and I know I do.

CHAPTER 26
TOGA

My mind is buzzing as I try to process everything my mom is saying. As much as I hate the woman, I believe her. Maybe that's a mistake. Maybe it's not. I don't know. But it's not something I'm going to figure out in the next few minutes. And not something I need to worry about while Ben is still out there somewhere, watching, waiting.

I glance at Fallon and see she's buying what my mother's selling. Hook, line, and sinker. She looks at me with sympathy and while I'd love to say I don't want it, it feels good to have her by my side.

"Toga, maybe you should call Magic," she suggests. "We have no—"

A knock echoes through the room. "Speak of the devil," I mutter as I walk to answer it.

I pull open the door and my eyes widen when I see Magic standing there with a pissed off look on his face and Ben behind him with a gun pointed at his head.

"Well, well, isn't this cozy," Ben quips. He shoves Magic into the room, causing him to stumble toward Fallon and my mom. At least that got the gun off his head. "The whole family, back together again."

"We're not a family," I growl. "Never have been, never will be."

Ben closes the door by kicking it, never taking his eyes off the rest of us. He focuses on his daughter.

"I gotta tell ya, Fallon, I was right about that guy." He nods to indicate Magic. "He's worthless. Got the drop on him as soon as he walked into his room."

"It was an ambush," Magic argues hotly. "Of course you got the drop on me. Had you come at me like a man, you wouldn't be standing."

"Magic, it's fine," I tell him, hoping to diffuse the situation. I want Magic angry, but not outwardly so. At least not until the time is right, like right before we take Ben's life.

"I know it's fine," Magic counters. "But this guy is pissing me the fuck off, Toga. Not only did he ambush me, but he also drank all the booze out of my mini fridge and dug through my luggage." Magic points to a lump on his head. "Oh, and let's not forget this. Fucker cold-cocked me."

"That bump on your head won't matter when you're six feet under," Ben tells him. His tone is calm, collected... goddamn annoying. "Now, on to business. Where's my money? I know it isn't in either hotel room. I checked."

"You don't listen, do you?" Fallon snaps, taking a step toward her father. "You're not getting a penny from me. And you're certainly not getting any from Satan's Legacy either."

As soon as Ben lifts his foot to take a step closer to her, I pull my gun from my waistband and point it at him. "That's close enough," I warn.

Ben laughs outright. He actually throws his head back and laughs like he doesn't have a care in the world.

"You're not gonna kill me." Ben swings his gun my way. "Do you know how many times you threatened that when you were younger? So many, I lost count. But what did you end up doing? You ran like a bitch. When it matters most, your balls disappear. So, please, put the gun down."

It goes against every instinct I have to listen to him. But I also don't want a full-blown shootout in the hotel. That'll just attract attention... and cops. We definitely don't need cops.

I lower my weapon but keep it in my hand, just in case. "There. Your turn."

"I don't think so."

"Whatever." I shrug like it's just another day at the office to have a gun pointing directly at me. I quickly glance at Fallon. "Hey, can you get my bottle of water out of your bag for me? No sense in adding cottonmouth to my list of complaints about this reunion."

Fallon looks at me for a moment, and I start to wonder if she understands. I don't give a flying fuck about water. What I do care about is that knife she put in there this morning. Since we can't get to the weapons in Magic's room, we'll have to use what we have access to. Finally, she breaks eye contact and shifts her gaze to Magic as she takes a few steps toward her bag.

All hell breaks loose.

With Ben distracted as he watches Fallon, I launch myself at him. We both go crashing to the floor. He lands a cheap shot to my face, but I deliver two to his. I hear Margaret scream in the background and can only hope she shuts up because that will draw unwanted attention too.

Magic and Fallon's shoes come into my peripheral.

While I'm delivering blow by blow, I can feel their eyes on me, watching my every move and likely wanting to trade places.

"You sorry sack of shit." I spit in Ben's face as I straighten, although I remain straddled on top of him in case he tries to get up. "You think you can walk all over people, ruin their lives and beat them down, literally, and you're still gonna come out on top." I spit at him again. "Fuck you. Not on my watch."

Ben swipes at the blood on his mouth and grins. "So you keep saying. And yet, here I am, still breathing."

That's it. Time to get this over with. I can't stand to look at this guy for another minute. I don't care how it happens or who does it but he's gotta die... now.

I stand and haul him to his feet. Shoving him against the wall, I pin him there.

"Got that water, baby?" I ask Fallon.

She lifts the knife for me to see. "Yep."

"You tell me what you want. I can end this now or let you get revenge first. Up to you."

"Oh, I'm ending this, but I think Magic gets a turn too. After being ambushed and all."

"Damn right I do," Magic agrees.

"Fine." I push away from Ben but stay close. "You've got two minutes. I want him alive for Fallon."

Magic bends to pull the long serrated knife he has sheathed at his ankle. The one he always carries. For a moment, I worry he's not going to listen and kill the bastard, but he surprises me.

"Trade ya."

He holds his knife out to Fallon and she stares at it a moment as if weighing her options. Being the smart woman she is, she takes what he's offering and slaps her own knife into his palm.

Magic then starts taking all of his pent-up rage out on Ben. He thrusts the knife anywhere in Ben's body that he knows won't cause death. He keeps at it until Ben's blood soaks his clothes and he's barely hanging on.

"Enough," I bark and Magic stops.

When he turns to me, his mouth is pulled into a giant grin. "Thanks. I needed that."

With that, he goes to stand next to Margaret, who's stopped screaming but is now silently sobbing.

"Ready?" I ask Fallon.

She looks at the blade gleaming in her hand before thrusting it into Ben's stomach. "More than ready."

Because Ben is barely able to stand, I pull him away from the wall and hold him in front of me so she has a clear target. Fallon yanks the blade out of his body, only to thrust it back in, over and over again.

"This is for my mom." Stab, stab, stab. "And this is for all the other women you've hurt during your miserable life." Stab, stab. "And this, you bottom-feeding mother-fucker, is for me." Stab, stab, stab, stab.

Fallon continues her assault and while he's clinging to life, Ben gurgles as he tries to laugh. Blood coats his teeth and dribbles down his chin. I'm holding him up as he's no longer able to stand at all.

"F-Fallon?" His voice is barely audible but it's enough to make her slow down and look at him.

"What?"

"There's o-one more thing y-you sh-should know," he pushes out. My body tenses because what more could he possibly say or do to her? I lean around to look at his face and see his crimson smirk. "I'm not y-your f-father."

That was not what I was expecting and judging by Fallon's wide-eyed expression, neither was she. She manages to maintain her composure and hits him with a smile.

"Thank God for that." Fallon grasps Ben by the back of his neck and pulls him toward her. At the same time, she presses the tip of the blade into his chest, right over his heart. She leans in close and whispers. "Go to Hell, motherfucker."

Ben lets out a groan when Fallon forces the knife through to pierce his heart. As soon as the hilt hits his flesh, she collapses to the floor, utterly exhausted.

Both Magic and my mother rush forward. Margaret drops to her knees next to Fallon and Magic takes over to move Ben's body to the bathtub so I can focus on my girl.

I scoop Fallon up in my arms and cradle her as I carry her to the bed. When I lay her on the mattress, she latches onto my shirt and pulls me down with her.

"Is it really over?"

"Yeah, Kid, it's really over."

CHAPTER 27

FALLON

"Yeah, we're on our way home. Only a few hours away."

I listen to Magic talking on the phone while I stare out the passenger window and watch the trees whiz by. I know I should probably try to get some sleep, but I don't want to. I'm alive. My villain has been defeated, and I can move forward without constantly watching over my shoulder. Life is good. Too good to sleep it away.

"Great," Magic says. I can't hear the other end of the conversation, but I imagine he's talking to Snow. "Yeah, sorry about that. Things got a little crazy." I glance over my shoulder and see him nodding. "I know. We're ready. Okay, later."

Magic ends the call and shoves his phone in the pocket of his cut. He looks everywhere around him but at me. And the sly smile he's trying to hide tells me he's up to something. I just don't know what.

"Everything good with Snow?" Toga asks.

"Last I talked to him, yeah."

"Dude, you just got off the phone with him."

"Oh, yeah, that was Laney."

"Laney? Why are you talking to Laney?"

I think I have an idea, but I keep my mouth shut. It's not my secret to share. Besides, Toga would know if Magic wanted him to.

"I guess Snow made her the point person for us until we get home. He had a few runners he wanted to see in action, and they all had drops today."

Toga looks confused but seems to accept his explanation.

"Well, what did Laney have to say?" he asks when it seems Magic isn't going to voluntarily provide any more information.

"She confirmed that the local chapter of Satan's Legacy, or the closest one, took care of the body and the hotel rooms. They also wiped the security footage so no worries there. She said she spoke to your mother and her plane arrived safely in Connecticut. Other than that, she warned that Snow wants a full debriefing when we get home, so we better be prepared."

"Any updates from Brady?" I ask, unable to sit by any longer and be patient.

"No." Magic shakes his head. "Not yet. She said he's working on it though. Brady should have confirmation within a few days as to whether or not you're biologically related to Ben."

"Okay."

When Ben told me he wasn't my father, I panicked, but only for a split second. Then I realized that was the best news of my life. Whether or not he was telling the truth is another story.

Toga reaches across the console, grabs my hand, and

squeezes. "And if he was telling the truth, we'll find out who your real father is. I promise."

There's that word again: promise. Over the last two months Toga has thrown that word out there like it's nothing. But it isn't nothing. Not to me. Toga has also done the unexpected. He's kept his promises, fulfilled them in every way. It used to piss me off when he promised things. Now, I've come to appreciate it.

"Thanks." I inhale deeply and blow out the breath. "Is it wrong of me to hope he's not my father?"

"No," Toga says. "He's evil and I imagine it's relieving to know there's a chance that his blood doesn't run through your veins."

"Kinda like it's relieving to know your mom isn't completely against you?"

Toga's face falls. "Yeah, something like that."

"Jesus, the mood in this car has tanked," Magic complains. "I, for one, don't want to be depressed right now and you're both killing my vibe. We should be celebrating the fact that that scumbag isn't breathing anymore. We should be celebrating your freedom from him and his reign of terror. And for fuck's sake, we should be celebrating the two of you. You finally get to begin the happily ever after you've wanted for eight years."

Toga smiles at me. "Asshole's annoying, but he's got a point."

I shift in my seat and sit a little straighter. "Agreed. No more talk about the things we can't control. Or about the things that will take time to process and emotionally work through." I look at Magic over my shoulder. "So, bro, what'd you have in mind?"

"Hell, I don't know." Magic chuffs out a breath. "We're in a fucking car! Not sure there's much celebrating to be done until we get home." He snaps his fingers. "Oh, shit, wait." Magic spins around and digs through a bag in the cargo area. When he turns back around, he's got a joint between his fingers. "I forgot I had this."

I stare at his idea of celebrating and for a moment, I contemplate yelling at him. But then I realize that life is short. Sometimes you have to bend the rules so you can really live. Sometimes you have to take the leap and trust that you'll land on your feet.

Don't get me wrong, I'm not a prude. In fact, any time I get together with Laney or Sami, weed is usually involved. Weed or alcohol. I'm quite fond of a little puff, puff, pass. The leap comes in when you're in a moving vehicle, in a state where the shit isn't legal, and you just don't care.

"Looks like a celebration to me," I say, reaching for the joint.

Before handing it to me, Magic lights it and takes a hit. He passes it to me and when I'm done, I do the same with Toga.

He hesitates for a moment and then caves. "I'm in." He takes a long drag before handing it over his shoulder to Magic.

Once the joint is smoked, the vibe in the Jeep is completely different than earlier. We're all singing along to the music, laughing our asses off at stupid shit, and genuinely enjoying one another's company.

I'd love to say all the other crap that was still weighing us down disappeared. I can't though because it didn't. It'll never disappear until we're ready to let it. But until then, I'm choosing to focus on the good: my friends, my new family, Toga.

I lean back against the passenger door and watch as he drives. I soak up the image of him expertly weaving in and out of traffic, the side glances he throws my way, his smile, and even the frustration he displays when other driver's piss him off. I do it because it's the final piece to the story of my life.

My man, my biker, taking me where I've always wanted to go: home.

EPILOGUE

TOGA

Six months later...

"We're gonna be late!"

I grin into the mirror and revel in the fact that Fallon's voice never gets old. Even when she's yelling at me, I want to hear it. My time with her so far has been everything I hoped for and more. It hasn't been without pitfalls, but we navigate them together, as a team.

Fallon's face appears in the mirror as she rushes through the doorway. "Did you hear me? We're gonna be late for the party."

Source of Love opens tomorrow in Denver, so tonight, Satan's Legacy is throwing an exclusive party for Fallon. No outsiders will be allowed at the clubhouse, and we will be charging a cover fee. Yes, we're charging our members for entry, for booze too, because all of the proceeds are going toward the non-profit. There's not a brother in this club who won't shell out a few bills.

When I turn to look at Fallon so I can really see *her* and *not* her reflection, my cock immediately reacts. I try to keep my gaze on her face, but the tight jeans and black leather halter top make it impossible. Add in the fuck me biker boots and she's going to have to resign herself to being late.

I scoop her up and throw her over my shoulder to carry her like a sack of potatoes to the bed. She's the food, and I'm a starving man.

"Toga," she cries with a laugh in her tone. "I can't be late to my own party."

"How much time do we have?" I ask as I toss her on the bed and watch her tits bounce.

"Less than ten minutes."

I start stripping off my clothes.

"Give me five."

My shirt hit's the floor, followed by my jeans. When Fallon sees that I'm free balling it, her pupils dilate. I expect her to wait for me to undress her, considering her pitiful attempt at pretending she doesn't want this, want *me*, but she doesn't wait.

Instead, she grabs my ass and yanks me forward. Her mouth swallows my dick, and my knees threaten to buckle. I went from total control to being a slave to my baser instincts.

As Fallon works wonders with her mouth, she rolls my balls around in her hands, intensifying every spark to my nerve endings. I fist my fingers in her hair and tug her head away from my body. When she looks up at me with hooded eyes, I almost thrust and fuck her mouth on my own.

"Stand up," I growl.

"But I wa—"

"Stand. Up."

Fallon rises to her feet, licking her lips as she does,

which causes me to question my sanity. She starts to kick her boots off, but I kneel down and take them off for her. Then I hook my thumbs in her waistband and yank them off her legs, leaving her wet pussy free for me to do with as I please.

I could easily lean in and end this in the few minutes she said we had but I'm not looking for quick. Fuck the party.

I stand to my full height and untie the halter top, throwing it to the floor when it's free. Her nipples are erect and begging to be lavished but I hold off on that too.

"Toga, we don't have ti—"

I shove two fingers into her folds, thrusting them in and out. "We have time."

Fallon throws her head back on a moan and I continue to finger fuck her until the moment her pussy starts to spasm. Quickly removing them, I lick them clean while staring into her pleading eyes. I've never not let her finish, so I know she wasn't expecting that.

Lifting Fallon into my arms, I back her into the wall, hard. A grunt escapes her but when I brush her clit, it quickly turns to moans.

"Fuck me, Toga," she pleads and starts to undulate her hips. "I need to come."

"I'll fuck you when I'm ready. And you'll come when I say you can."

She slams her head back against the wall in frustration. I set her on her feet and kneel in front of her. I don't waste any time before lapping at her clit with my tongue. Slow circles alternate with fast swipes, all designed to make her squirm.

And squirm she does.

The drink in the taste of her, inhale the scent of her.

Giving her pleasure is enough to satisfy me, but I'm not settling for enough. I want spectacular.

"Ah, Toga, don't stop," she moans.

I stop. "Uh, uh, ah. Not yet." I rise to my feet and lift her once again to pin her to the wall. I lean in close and press my lips to her ear. "I'm going to fill you up now."

I thrust into her in one smooth stroke, pausing when my balls slap her skin, soaking up the feeling of doing exactly what I said I was going to do.

"Oh God." Fallon's head falls to my shoulder. "Oh fuck."

My hips fly and my muscles burn as I continue to impale her as hard and as fast as I can. Fallon's teeth sink into my flesh, and I know I'm not going to be able to hold her off any longer.

I feel a tingle race up my spine. "Okay, now, baby," I say from between clenched teeth.

On command, Fallon explodes. Her pussy quivers around me until I begin to pulse. We come together, as we so often do, but something about this time is different. It's hotter, better... epic.

When we're both panting, falling back down from the clouds, I carry her to the bathroom. We take the time to clean up, both of us quiet and soaking up what just happened.

I help Fallon get dressed and then put my own clothes back on. A quick glance at my phone tells me we definitely missed the beginning of the party.

"How late are we?"

"We're the perfect amount of late," I tell her.

Fallon swats my shoulder but smiles. "Is that what you're going to tell everyone else?"

I shrug. "Sure, why not?"

"I've gotta say, life with you is never dull." Fallon walks

out of the bedroom, to the kitchen, and grabs a bottle of water out of the fridge. I follow behind her. "Although, if that's what being late with you is like, I'll take it."

"Finally, you see things my way." I nuzzle her neck from behind before spinning her around to face me. "Wanna go another round and see if we can really make you late." I wink, hoping she catches my double meaning.

"We don't need to go another round."

Say what?

"I already am," she tacks on.

"Already are what?" I ask, sure I'm misreading the conversation.

"Late."

It's her turn to wink, and she lowers her hand to her still flat abdomen.

"About three weeks to be exact."

Next in the Satan's Legacy MC Series

Magic's Tormet

Magic...

As the Enforcer for Satan's Legacy MC, it's not my job to keep secrets. In fact, when someone does keep one from my club, I'm the guy who has to make them pay. And I love doling out the punishment for any crime committed against the club. It's exhilarating.

But now I'm the one with the secret... a freakin' doozy at that. I've managed to keep it to myself for a while, but like a ticking bomb, time is quickly running out. I need to spill my guts knowing that it may result in my guts literally being spilled and the end of my life as I know it. That's a chance I'm willing to take... for *her*.

Laney...

As the baby sister of the Satan's Legacy MC president, I'm always under constant scrutiny. Sure, they call it 'protection', but it's smothering. Because I'm not only a sister.

I'm a mother, a friend, and a steel vault when it comes to details about a certain aspect of my personal life.

But when a ghost from the past crawls out of the grave, that steel vault melts with each passing day until it disappears, and my son and I are left more vulnerable than we've ever been. And the one person who has broken every single club code has no choice but to come clean and risk his life. The problem is, I want to protect *him,* even if it means breaking my own heart and giving up my life in the process.

ABOUT THE AUTHOR

Andi Rhodes is an author whose passion is creating romance from chaos in all her books! She writes MC (motorcycle club) romance with a generous helping of suspense and doesn't shy away from the more difficult topics. Her books can be triggering for some so consider yourself warned. Andi also ensures each book ends with the couple getting their HEA! Most importantly, Andi is living her real life HEA with her husband and their boxers.

For access to release info, updates, and exclusive content, be sure to sign up for Andi's newsletter at andirhodes.com.

Also by Andi Rhodes

Broken Rebel Brotherhood

Broken Souls

Broken Innocence

Broken Boundaries

Broken Rebel Brotherhood: Complete Series Box set

Broken Rebel Brotherhood: Next Generation

Broken Hearts

Broken Wings

Broken Mind

Bastards and Badges

Stark Revenge

Slade's Fall

Jett's Guard

Soulless Kings MC

Fender

Joker

Piston

Greaser

Riker

Trainwreck

Squirrel

Gibson

Satan's Legacy MC

Snow's Angel

Toga's Demons

Magic's Torment

Printed in Great Britain
by Amazon

44178515R00118